BOARDING PASS
PASSENGER TICKET AND BAGGAGE CHECK
FIRST CLASS
GATE
7
GATE CLOSES
19:30
SEAT
25b
Arrival
GATE:
7
GATE
CLOSES:
19:30
SEAT
25b
This nation has a banner . . . it is the
Every color means liberty;
banner of Dawn. It means
every thread means liberty
Visas
DEPARTMENT OF HOMELAND SECURITY • U.S. CUSTOMS AND BORDER PROTECTION
ADMITTED
ATL
JUL 18 2012
0890
AUG 16 2012
06 08.12 30
MADRID • BARAJAS
R
Gävle
Turku
Uppsala
Stockhol
Wrocław
Katowice
Prague
CH REP.
Vienna
Linz
STRIA
Ljubljana
Zagreb
CROAT
Split
Sea
Tirana
ALBANIA
Bari
Táranto
Thessaloniki
GREECE
Bursa

Rabbi Nosson Scherman / Rabbi Meir Zlotowitz
General Editors

SRES. MEDICOS
CUERPO NACIONAL DE POLICIA
Take Me
Published by
Mesorah Publications, ltd

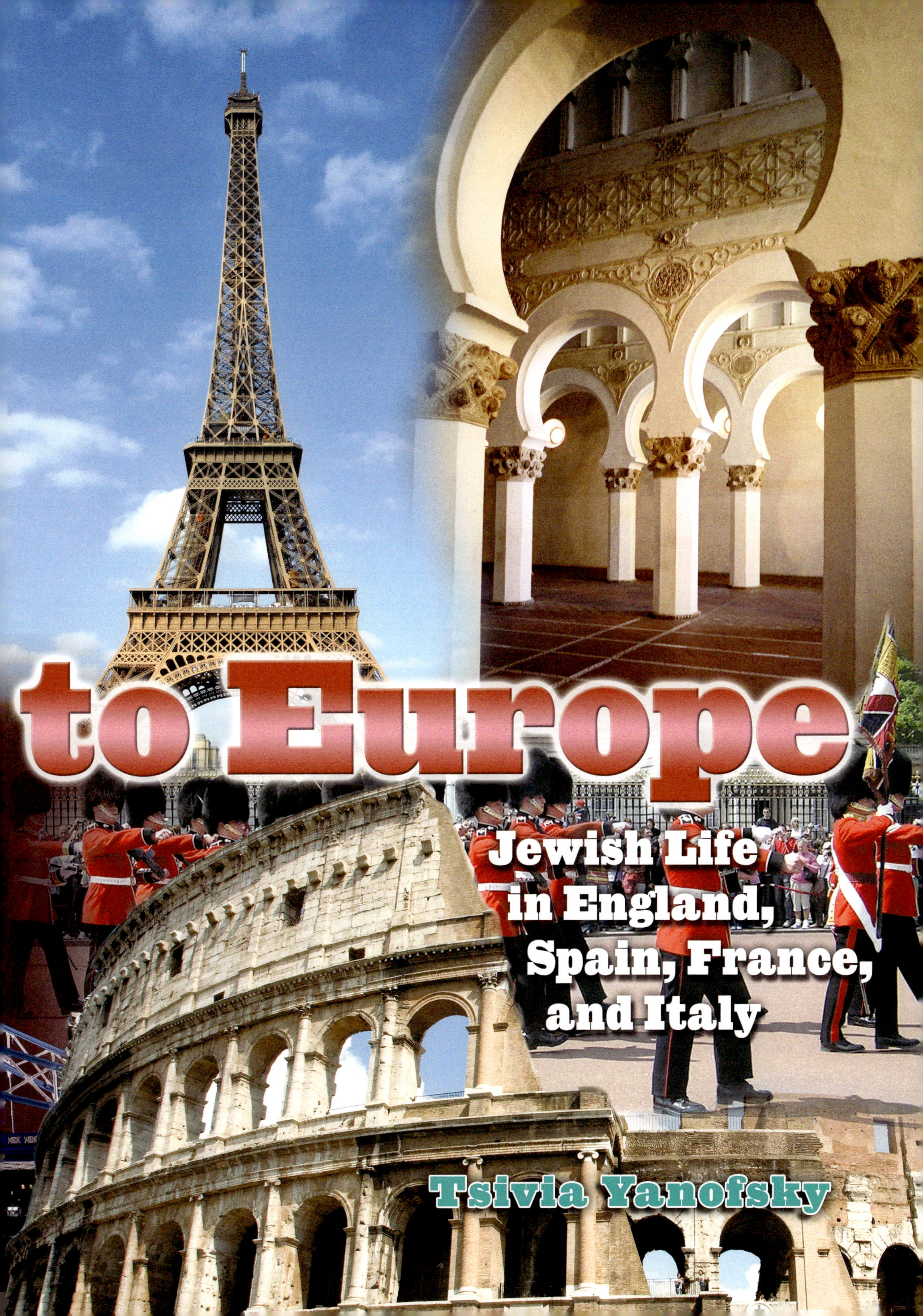
to Europe
Jewish Life in England, Spain, France, and Italy
Tsivia Yanofsky

TAKE ME TO EUROPE

First edition — First impression: February 2013

Published by **MESORAH PUBLICATIONS, LTD.**
4401 Second Avenue / Brooklyn, N.Y 11232 / (718) 921-9000 / Fax: (718) 680-1875
www.artscroll.com

Distributed in Israel by **SIFRIATI / A. GITLER**
6 Hayarkon Street / Bnei Brak 51127

Distributed in Europe by **LEHMANNS**
Unit E, Viking Business Park, Rolling Mill Road / Jarrow, Tyne and Wear / England NE32 3DP

Distributed in Australia and New Zealand by **GOLDS WORLD OF JUDAICA**
3-13 William Street / Balaclava, Melbourne 3183, Victoria, Australia

Distributed in South Africa by **KOLLEL BOOKSHOP**
Northfield Centre / 17 Northfield Avenue / Glenhazel 2192 / Johannesburg, South Africa

Printed in the United States of America by **Noble Book Press Corp.**
Custom bound by **Sefercraft, Inc.** / 4401 Second Avenue / Brooklyn N.Y. 11232

ISBN-10: 1-4226-1349-6 / ISBN-13: 978-1-4226-1349-8

PHOTO CREDITS

Classical Numismatic Group, Inc.
http://www.cngcoins.com — page 66

Jon Bennett — page 33 (bottom)

Joel and Linda Berkowitz — pages 56, 76

Steve F-E-Cameron — page 30 (bottom)

Mathieu CHAINE — page 57 (bottom)

Pam Fray — page 13

Grunfeld family — page 29 (left)

iStockphoto — page 27 (bottom-right) 66 (background)

Asmus Koefoed — page 58 (top)

Eli Kroen — page 27 (top)

NASA — page — 30 (top)

Photo8 — page 49 (bottom)

Abby Sanfield — page 34

C.J. Schitzler — page 17 (top)

Eliyahu Saftlas — page 27 (bottom-left, middle-left)

Thinkstock — pages 7, 14 (bottom), 15, 16, 17 (bottom), 18, 19, 20, 21, 22, 23 (botom), 28 (bottom), 29, 30 (bottom), 31, 32 (bottom), 33 (top), 36, 38, 39, 40, 41, 42, 46, 47, 50, 51, 52, 53, 54, 55, 57 (bottom), 58 (bottom), 59, 60, 61, 62, 68, 69, 70, 71, 72, 73, 74, 75, 78, 79, 81 (top), 83, 88 (pictures 1, 4), 89 (pictures 6, 7)

Wikimedia Commons — pages 14 (top), 23 (top), 25 (top), 30 (bottom), 80, 81 (bottom), 88 (pictures 2, 3), 89 (pictures 5, 8)

Yanofsky family — page 48 (bottom)

Moshe D. Yarmish — pages 24, 25 (bottom-left)

CONTENTS

This book, Take Me to Europe, *is dedicated to the one and half million European Jewish children who were murdered in the Holocaust. European soil absorbed their blood and bore silent witness to their pain. May Hashem avenge their deaths. It is my prayer that Jewish children the world over merit to run and play in the streets of Yerushalayim, with the arrival of Mashiach.*

Acknowlegements

First and foremost, I offer שֶׁבַח וְהוֹדָאָה to Hashem for providing me with a forum to enlighten and inspire Jewish children with knowledge of their history and heritage.

I would like to thank my beloved parents and in-laws for their unstinting support for this project as well as for so many of my life's endeavors. My children, who are involved in many of my projects and activities, provided some keen insights that I incorporated into this book. My *talmidos,* as well, are a tremendous source of inspiration. Above all, my husband, Shimon, is my guide and partner in all of my pursuits. His dedication to *tinokos shel bais rabban* is legendary. May we merit to see much *nachas* from our children.

A very special thank-you to my brother, R' Yecheskel Silberstein for his keen insights. He is a master editor and a terrific brother.

A special thank-you, as well, to Rabbi Zvi Belsky, a noted *talmid chacham* and scholar, for his insights.

Thank you to Dina Spilzburger, a talented graphic artist, for impacting the initial design of this book.

As always it was an absolute pleasure to publish a book with ArtScroll/Mesorah Publications, whose hallmark of excellence is world renowned. The photo layout and graphic design are truly challenging and could only be achieved by a devoted and exceptionally talented staff such as that at ArtScroll/Mesorah Publications. My great appreciation to Rabbi Nosson Scherman and Rabbi Meir Zlotowitz, who are at the helm of this remarkable publishing company. I greatly appreciate the devoted efforts of Mendy Herzberg, who masterfully coordinated and produced this book, Eli Kroen for the magnificent cover design, and Devorah Bloch, whose book design demonstrates great talent. Thank you to Mimi Zakon, a master editor who hails from the Holy Land, and to Felice Eisner, a master onsite editor and proofreader.

May ArtScroll continue to succeed in all of its endeavors.

Dear Reader,

Do you ever dream of "going abroad" and visiting countries in Europe? Do you want to explore new places and see history come alive? Paris, London, Madrid, and Rome are beautiful cities with magnificent palaces, winding streets, and interesting landmarks. When you read a book, you can be magically transported to another place and even another era.

So sit back, fasten your "seatbelts," and relax. I hope that this book enriches you in some way. Most of all, I hope that it deepens your appreciation for your rich heritage — wherever you live and whoever you are.

Sincerely,

Your author,

Tsivia Yanofsky

Dear Parents...

For thousands of years, nations have risen and fallen, sometimes disappearing without a trace of their former glory. How did we, the Jewish nation, maintain ourselves for so many centuries? We were enslaved, downtrodden, and oppressed. Ever since we existed as a nation, other nations have tried to annihilate us: The Egyptians, Babylonians, Medes and Persians, Greeks and Romans in the ancient world; in modern times the Germans, the Soviets, the Arabs, and now, the latest in a long line of bloodthirsty enemies, the Iranians. They have forced us into slavery, confined us within ghettos, robbed and murdered us. And yet, despite everything we remain the King's son.

What is the secret of our existence? How do we maintain our nobility and dignity in a corrupt world? Our secret lies in one word — Torah. The teachings of Hashem as taught in our holy Torah ensure our survival as a nation.

The seventy nations of the world and their offshoots have tried to destroy us. Seventy wolves have stalked one pure and innocent sheep. At times, the wolves scratched at the sheep, causing it to bleed profusely, staining the ground crimson with its blood. But always, always the Shepherd came to the rescue, snatching the little sheep from the wolves in the nick of time.

We are now at the end of the last and most difficult exile, *malchus Edom*. Our *gedolim* call this time, *Ikveseh D'mshicha*. We will hear the footsteps of Mashiach if we listen carefully. David HaMelech tells us, "יָבֹאוּ וְיַגִּידוּ צִדְקָתוֹ לְעַם נוֹלָד כִּי עָשָׂה" (*Tehillim* 22:32). The last generation of exiles will tell over the righteousness of Hashem and His salvation to the new generation who never knew of exiles and sufferings. It is the hope and prayer of this author that this book be read by such children. Children who never heard of death and suffering. Children who will play and run in the streets of Yerushalayim. And we will tell them of Hashem's wonders.

We will tell them what this world was like. They will listen, wide-eyed, as we describe the United States, Europe, Australia, and the Middle East and all that happened over the generations. We will tell them about momentous events, about the Spanish Exile, the crematoria of Auschwitz, the blood libels of England, the burning of the Talmud in France. But most of all, we will tell them that we held the torch for them. We kept the connection to the *gedolim* of the previous generations, to the Bartenoro, Sforno, Rambam, Ramban, the great scholars of the past mentioned in this book. We held on tight and we were Hashem's emissaries in this world. We were refined, honest, and princely. And we accomplished this only by adhering to our holy Torah.

We erected shuls and *batei midrash*, yeshivos and Jewish homes, *al taharos hakodesh*. Yes, even in exile. It is because of us, because of our love of Hashem and His holy Torah that the nation of Klal Yisrael continued to exist. And Hashem, our Shepherd, our Father, protected and guarded us. Even when the nations threatened to wipe us off the face of the earth, He did not forsake us. He allowed us to rebuild and blossom once again. His holy *Shechinah* accompanied us from one exile to another. And we always knew that one day He would bring us back home. And there in our ancestral home, Eretz Yisrael, we would serve Hashem in purity and in joy. We would learn His holy Torah, which was the light of our eyes and a balm to our souls even in the darkest days of exile.

England shares the island of Great Britain with Scotland and Wales.

ENGLAND

The History of the Jews in England

Until *Churban Bayis Sheini*, the destruction of the Second *Beis HaMikdash*, most Jews lived in and near Eretz Yisrael. After the *Beis HaMikdash* was destroyed, Jews were scattered all over Europe, Asia, and Africa.

Some Jews lived in England after the *Churban Beis HaMikdash*, but they did not become an organized community until the year 1066. Often, the Jews of England were hated and persecuted by the non-Jews. In the year 1144, Jews in Norwich, England were accused of murder. A rumor sprang up that a Christian child had been kidnapped by Jews and killed. In the years that followed there were more accusations against the Jews. One type of accusation was called a "blood libel," when non-Jews accused Jews of killing Christian children for their blood. It sounds ridiculous and silly, but unfortunately many non-Jews believed it. Many Jews were killed because of blood libels.

Finally, in 1296 the Jews were banished from England. Their houses and properties went to the king. The Jews were banned from England for over 350 years, until the seventeenth century.

Two Great Jews

Rav Manashe Ben Israel was a *talmid chacham* who lived in Portugal and later in Amsterdam. Oliver Cromwell was a powerful English military and political leader at the time. In 1656, Rav Manashe succeeded in convincing Cromwell, who was sympathetic to the Jews, to allow the Jews to reenter England. This was a very big accomplishment as Jews had been banished from England for over 350 years!

The Jews greatly appreciated the kindness that Oliver Cromwell showed them.

The Jewish nation did not have many friends among the nations throughout its long and bitter exile. Any friend it did have was greatly appreciated. One example was Alexander the Great, who conquered much of the world. Some wicked non-Jews who lived in Eretz Yisrael sent a message to Alexander. They falsely accused the Jews of rebelling against the king. When Alexander came to Eretz Yisrael the Jews sent the Kohen Gadol, Shimon HaTzaddik, to greet the mighty Alexander. When Alexander saw Shimon HaTzaddik, he got off his horse and bowed down before him. The soldiers with him were shocked. Alexander explained that before he was successful in battles he always saw an image of an old man with a beard. That man, he now realized, was Shimon HaTzaddik! He told Shimon HaTzaddik that the Jews had his full permission to do as they saw fit to the anti-Semites. There is a tradition that, forever grateful for the kindness of Alexander, Jewish boys born that year were named Alexander. Until today Alexander (which is sometimes shortened to Sender) is a name given to Jewish babies at their bris. Klal Yisrael never forgets its friends, few and far between as they are.

In the 1600's, after Cromwell allowed the Jews to return to England and practice their faith, many Jews from Holland, Spain, and Portugal came to England. England became one of the countries in Europe that was more tolerant to Jews.

Two hundred years later, in the 1800's, another great Jew, a Sephardic immigrant by the name of **Moses (Moshe) Montefiore**, arrived in England. He worked together with Baron Rothschild, who was his brother-in-law. By the age of thirty Montefiore had become fabulously wealthy. Although he was very young, he decided to retire and to devote the rest of his life to helping other Jews. Montefiore had great influence with Queen Victoria and often protected Jews in danger. He loved Eretz Yisrael and helped build up and restore many of the holy places in Eretz Yisrael, including Kever Rachel. He also helped the struggling, poverty-stricken Jews in Eretz Yisrael. Sir Moses built a settlement and a windmill that he thought would help the Jews of Yerushalayim earn a living. The windmill never worked well, but it became a symbol of his charity and kindness.

Montefiore's grave in Ramsgate, England, patterned after Kever Rachel, which he rebuilt.

The Tower of London

Built in the eleventh century, the name "Tower of London" would send shivers up even a royal spine. In the 1200's six hundred Jews were imprisoned in the Tower of London. Two hundred seventy of them were hanged by order of the king. Later, Henry the Eighth, a cruel English king, imprisoned his wife, the queen, in this tower.

The British Crown Jewels, including the state crown, are displayed in the Tower of London.

Did you know that modern postage stamps were invented in Britain in 1840?

The first stamp was called the "Penny Black."

Her Majesty's State Crown

Stars and Stripes "Forever"?

The British flag is known as the Union Jack. The original version was flown on ships in the 1600's.

In the 1600's and 1700's, settlers from England and other European countries founded the thirteen colonies on the eastern coast of what is now the United States. Many colonists came in search of new homes or a chance to earn a living. Others, including many Jews, wanted religious freedom. The original thirteen colonies grew and grew. On July 4, 1776, they declared their independence from England and formed their own country, called the United States of America. As a result of these beginnings, many American traditions have English roots. One of the most important is representative government, the right to elect the people who govern us.

On every Fourth of July, Americans celebrate their freedom, which was proclaimed in the Declaration of Independence. John Hancock's signature is very large on the original Declaration of Independence; it was later said that he didn't want the King of England to need glasses to read it.

American Jews are grateful to a nation that allows us freedom to worship Hashem according to the laws of our Holy Torah. About twenty-five years before the Revolutionary War, Rav Chaim Volozhiner famously said, "The last stop of the *galus* will be America."

Let us daven that we will soon all leave the "last stop" to go to our Holy Land, when Mashiach arrives.

Did you know that in England you drive on the left-hand side of the road, and the car's steering wheel is on the right?

Translating English into English

Many words that are common in England have to be "translated" for Americans. Here are some of them:

British English		American English
jumper	=	sweater
chemist	=	drugstore
fortnight	=	two weeks
gaol	=	jail (but pronounced the same way)
lift	=	elevator
lorry	=	truck
nappy	=	diaper
Mummy	=	Mommy
boot	=	trunk of a car
flat	=	apartment
football	=	soccer

Looks Like Rain

England is famous for its cool, damp weather. Clouds start to form quickly, turning blue skies into gray. Although England is known for its fog, rain, and umbrellas, the rainfalls do not actually add up to much rain, as showers are mostly light and brief.

Did you know that England is on the same latitude as Newfoundland, Canada? But while Newfoundland faces very cold winters, England's are milder. This is because of the Gulf Stream, a big ocean current that carries warm water from the Caribbean Sea to the British coast.

Big Ben and a Little Sundial: Two Fascinating Clocks

Britain's capital city, London, is home to some of the world's most recognizable landmarks. One of these is the enormous clock tower nicknamed Big Ben. Built in 1858, it is 316 feet tall – that's 31 stories high! To get to the top you have to climb 334 stairs (whew!). The clock's mechanism is amazing and has only broken down once or twice since it was built. Even during World War II, when London was bombed heavily, the clock tower was hit, but Big Ben kept time correctly. But don't try to carry that clock mechanism away — it weighs five full tons!

On Jaffa Street in Yerushalayim, near the city's famous Machane Yehudah shuk, the open-air market, is a much smaller clock, that has a very different history. It is built on top of a shul called Zoharei Chamah, which means "Shinings of the Sun." It is not an ordinary clock, it is a sundial, an instrument that shows time by the shadow of the pointer cast by the sun onto a dial. The sundial was built by Reb Moshe Shapiro, a watchmaker in Yerushalayim, who taught himself science and astronomy by studying the sefarim of the Rambam and the Vilna Gaon. Reb Moshe built several sundials in Yerushalayim, including one for the famous Churvah Shul, one for Zoharei Chamah, and one for the Gra Shul of Shaarei Chesed.

Reb Moshe's sundials attracted the attention of the local Muslim Waqf, or ruler, who wished to install one on the Har HaBayis. Reb Moshe refused, as it is forbidden for a Jew to go onto the Har HaBayis. When the Waqf continued to pressure him, he turned to Harav Yosef Chaim Sonnenfeld, the Rav of Yerushalayim. The Rav suggested that he ask for an outrageously large sum of money, hoping that the Waqf would back down. Unfortunately this did not stop the Waqf, who was very wealthy. Rav Shapiro refused to take the money, even though it would have made him very rich. Rav Sonnenfeld then summoned several Muslim elders and persuaded them that it would not be right to cause a Jew to act against his belief. The Arabs who heard that the Jew had refused this job grew very angry, and Reb Moshe Shapiro was forced to leave Eretz Yisrael until things calmed down.

Big Ben looms high on the British horizon, but the small sundial near the *shuk* is really much greater. It shows that a Jew will refuse vast wealth, and will even go into exile, rather than do an *aveirah*.

London "Tower" Bridge

London Tower Bridge at night is truly a dazzling sight. In London, the capital city of England, the River Thames flows beneath the Tower Bridge. Tower Bridge has a roadway that opens to allow tall ships to pass through.

There are royal guards in Tanach too! In Megillas Esther, King Achashveirosh's guards, Bigsan and Seresh, plotted to kill the king. Their plot was foiled by Mordechai HaTzaddik.

Changing the Guard

Buckingham Palace in London is the main residence of the British Royal family. At 11:30 a.m., there is a changing of the guards in front of the palace gates. The new guard replaces the old guard during a ceremony that is very popular with tourists. These guardsmen are supposed to stand absolutely still, and they are not supposed to show any emotion at all. Some tourists have fun trying to make the guards laugh, but they are never successful. The guards are careful to follow royal orders.

There is a Rashi in Sefer Daniel that reminds us of this. On the words in Daniel that can be translated as "holding back from laughter," Rashi says that this refers to men who stand before the king. It is amazing to see that everything is contained in the Torah and the words of our chachamim.

England is a nation surrounded by the sea. No place in England is more than seventy-five miles from the ocean. Although England is small, only a little larger than the state of Louisiana, it has many different kinds of scenery. It has mountains, valleys, marshlands, moors, big lakes, plains, and cliffs. Cornwall in Western England is famous for its rugged cliffs.

Many fields in England are enclosed by rows of bushes called hedgerows. Hedgerows line many of the narrow roads in the British countryside.

Feed the Birds

Britain's cities are home to many pigeons. They were once raised for food, but now they live wild. Tourists used to enjoy feeding the pigeons in places like Trafalgar Square. This has now been banned, as London is trying to get rid of the pesky pigeons. Trafalgar Square is also famous for another reason. Anybody can stand up there and give a public speech.

A Kiddush Hashem in the House of Lords

Rabbi Immanuel Jakobovits

Very few of us can hope to make a *Kiddush Hashem* among tens of millions of people. Rabbi Immanuel Jakobovits was one of the few who actually did so. Rabbi Jakobovits was the Chief Rabbi of the British Commonwealth. He was also famous worldwide as the first rabbi ever appointed to the House of Lords. (In England, instead of having a Senate and a House of Representatives, there is a House of Commons, whose members are elected, and a House of Lords, who are appointed by the Queen or King of England.) But Rabbi Jakobovits never felt that being in the House of Lords was as important to him as being a Rav. He visited the House of Lords but his home was the *bais midrash* and the *shul*. His speeches in the House of Lords were always based on true Jewish beliefs. He was widely admired as a brilliant thinker and as a fine person. When speaking to *frum* Yidden he often spoke about the fact that we cannot be ordinary people. We must be an exceptional people, a light to the nations. At a dinner honoring him upon his retirement, Margaret Thatcher, the Prime Minister of England, said, “Leadership of any kind in any age is lonely. But today you are not alone .... For among those of all faith and of none, you have secured the country’s esteem and affection.”

England has thirty-nine separate police forces. The most advanced police force is called Scotland Yard, familiar to readers of the Sherlock Holmes stories. Scotland Yard is called in by any of the other police forces when they need help solving a case. Policemen in England are called bobbies.

Did you know that Sir Winston Churchill was one of the most famous Englishmen of the twentieth century?

He was the prime minister during World War II. He was known as one of the greatest speakers of his time, and his inspiring speeches raised the hopes of millions during the Second World War. When somebody speaks using a rich and beautiful English, we say that he speaks "Churchillian English."

On workdays about six million people ride the double-decker buses in London.

Rav Dessler

When a Torah Jew thinks of England he thinks of **Rav Eliyahu Eliezer Dessler**, author of the famous *sefer Michtav Me'Eliyahu.* The Chazon Ish called Rav Dessler "the *gadol hador* in Torah thought."

Rav Dessler moved to England before World War II. At the outbreak of the war, he lost contact with his family, who had remained in Europe. Although after some time he learned that his wife and children were safe, the family was not reunited until the end of the war. During those years he showed tremendous self-control. Though of course he was very worried about his wife and children, he used every waking moment to build up the Torah life of England. He was hard at work in London arranging places to stay for yeshivah students who had arrived in London, escaping the Nazis. He ended every lecture he gave during those hard times with the question: "Why did Hashem allow us to live?" He was hinting to those who heard him that they must do everything they could to save Jewish lives and preserve the study and practice of Torah.

Although it seemed a terrible time to start a kollel, Rav Dessler, with his clear vision, understood otherwise. He joined Reb Dovid Dryan to establish the Gateshead Kollel, where some of the finest *talmidei chachamim* were able to learn. Rav Dessler knew that it is only with the power of Torah and *talmidei chachamim* that our nation will continue to survive.

There were some people who thought Rav Dessler was wrong to start a kollel and encourage young men to learn Torah during such terrible times. They did not realize that perhaps it was in the merit of *tzaddikim* and *talmidei chachamim* like Rav Dessler that London was not destroyed during the war. They forgot that when Avraham Avinu davened to Hashem not to destroy Sodom, Hashem said that He would not do so if there were fifty *tzaddikim* in the city. (Unfortunately, there weren't even ten *tzaddikim*, and Hashem did destroy Sodom.)

We too must realize that wherever we live, whether in America, Eretz Yisrael, Europe, Canada, Australia, or anywhere else in the world, we are protected from danger in the merit of the *tzaddikim* and *gedolim* in our midst. We must daven to Hashem to grant them long lives so that we can learn from their ways and enjoy their protection.

Yeshivos in England

The famed and prestigious Gateshead Yeshivah is located in the town of Gateshead in England. It is the largest yeshivah in Europe. The yeshivah was founded in Gateshead in 1929 and the Chafetz Chaim appointed the original heads of the yeshivah.

Harav Avrohom Gurwicz, current Rosh Yeshivah of Gateshead Yeshivah

Rav Matisyahu Salomon, former mashgiach in Gateshead Yeshivah, current Mashgiach of Lakewood Yeshivah

Rav Yehudah Zev Segal, the legendary Manchester Rosh Yeshivah, was raised in Manchester, England. Even in the great pre-war Mirrer Yeshivah he was a marvel of *hasmadah* and incredible growth in Torah and character development.

Many people would leave their businesses and yeshivos to go to Manchester for the *Yamim Noraim* to be in his presence. One of Rav Segal's legacies was bringing about an awareness of *shmiras halashon*, guarding one's speech. He promised that anyone who would learn two *shmiras halashon halachos* daily would have success or salvation.

Rav Yehudah Zev Segal, zt"l, the Manchester Rosh Yeshivah

The Manchester Yeshivah building

A Glance at the Past

For almost two thousand years after the *Churban,* hardly any Jews merited to live in Eretz Yisrael — then called Palestine. During the First World War, Britain captured it from the Turks, who lost the war. After the war, Britain was given the responsibility to oversee Palestine until it was ready for independence. Of course, the Jews wanted a Jewish nation in their homeland. The Arabs, on the other hand, were absolutely against the Jews returning. The British made promises to both sides, but in the end could not work out a compromise.

Britain became tired of the whole "Palestine issue," and at the end of World War II, it passed the problem to the United Nations, which had just been formed. The UN called for a partition, or dividing up, of the area into an Arab state and a Jewish state. Yerushalayim was to be an international city, not to be owned by either side.

We know that the hearts of kings and ministers are in the hands of Hashem. He guides all their decisions. A majority of the countries in the UN agreed: Part of Eretz Yisrael would be given, at last, to the Jews.

Though the Jews were not happy to divide Yerushalayim, they accepted the United Nations plan. The Arabs, though, refused. The date for the forming of the new State of Israel was set for May 14, 1948. The British pulled their soldiers out of Israel, and the infant state was on its own. That very night, six Arab states — Egypt, Iraq, Jordan, Lebanon, Saudi Arabia, and Syria —invaded Israel. The fighting was terrible and many Jews were killed or captured, but Hashem helped the Jews and Israel won the war.

We eagerly await the day when Hashem will bring all Jews back to our homeland, Eretz Yisrael, where we can enjoy the glory of Hashem's holy *Shechinah* and live in harmony and joy forever.

Visas Departures / Sorties Entrées Entrées

"Queen" of England

In 1938, the Nazis had taken over Austria and were bringing their horrors to Austrian Jews. Solomon Schonfeld, an energetic and brilliant young British rabbi, heard about the hundreds of Jewish children in Austria whose parents had been killed by the Nazis. Rabbi Schonfeld did all he could to get permission to bring the orphaned children to England. He even risked his own life to go to Austria and get them! That was only the first of what were called "Kindertransports" ("Kinder" is German for "children") brought into England by Rabbi Dr. Schonfeld. By the time the war ended, Rabbi Schonfeld had brought over 3,700 children into England!

Some of the children saved from the Nazis stayed with relatives who lived in England. Others lived in London in Rabbi Schonfeld's charge. In 1939, the Nazis began bombing England. The British government realized that London would be a major target. They decided to evacuate, or send to safety, all school children in London to small towns outside the city. There they would be safer.

Among them were 450 Jewish children; they were sent out of London under the loving care of Dr. Judith Grunfeld. Years before, Dr. Grunfeld had worked with Sarah Schenirer, who founded the Bais Yaakov movement. When Dr. Grunfeld moved to England, she became the head of Dr. Schonfeld's school.

As the children set out on this trip, two boys held a *Sefer Torah* at the head of the line. Wherever Jews go, whatever exile Hashem sends them to, the Torah goes with them. Dr. Grunfeld's young students were sent to the farming village of Shefford, where the local non-Jews opened their homes to the children. At first the non-Jews were very confused by their young visitors. Most of the host families had prepared large meals. There was ham, seafood, and nutritious meat. Everything looked delicious. Everything was *treif*! In house after house, the children shyly thanked their hosts and refused to eat anything besides vegetables. The hosts also looked forward to the children accompanying them to church. Of course the children wouldn't go. Some of the children couldn't even speak English. They spoke German, the language of the enemy.

Hashem helped and slowly but surely the children won over the non-Jewish families with their polite, gentle ways. Succahs, menorahs, and *tzitzis* all became common features in Shefford and the neighboring towns during the five years the children remained. Judith Grunfeld organized the entire operation and lovingly began to be called "The Queen." Dr. Grunfeld was truly regal and aristocratic.

When the author of this book was a young girl of twelve or thirteen "The Queen," Dr. Judith Grunfeld, came to Bais Yaakov of Borough Park to visit. The author clearly remembers an elegant woman whose presence generated much respect and excitement. Perhaps Dr. Grunfeld was called "the Queen" because she truly accepted upon herself the Kingship of the King of Kings.

Dr. Judith Grunfeld

Rabbi Dr. Solomon Schonfeld

Respect before the "King of Kings"

Queen Elizabeth II, the current Queen of England

Before a person meets Queen Elizabeth, the Queen of England, he receives special instructions. There is a special protocol, manner of behavior, which is required in the presence of Her Majesty. Even someone as important as the president of the United States must follow certain set rules when he meets the queen.

For example, when the Queen of England enters a cathedral or palace for a public event, all the people there rise to their feet. Eight gloriously uniformed trumpeters give her a festive fanfare and regal salute. When someone leaves her throne room, he ceremoniously walks out backwards, not turning his back to Her Majesty. If you are fortunate enough to visit the Royal Stables you will see magnificent horses and stunning old-fashioned gilded carriages that are still in use for occasions of state, such as a royal wedding.

So much awe and respect is required in the presence of the Queen, who is largely a figurehead, meaning that she doesn't have much power. How much more so must we have awe and respect when we pray before the King of Kings, *Melech Ha'Olam*, King of the entire world, who rules the heavens and the earth.

Every fall, Queen Elizabeth II opens the new session of Parliament. A horse-drawn carriage comes to Buckingham Palace to take the Queen to the Houses of Parliament. The current Queen has opened 53 sessions. This is one of the many traditions that are part of British life.

The Royal Observatory

The Royal Observatory was built at Greenwich, England, on the banks of the River Thames. An imaginary line runs through the Royal Observatory. It marks the 0° line of longitude, or the prime meridian. This is an imaginary line that circles the Earth from the North Pole to the South Pole. All distances from the east to the west are measured from this line.

England is divided into forty counties, or "shires." County names often end in "shire," as in Berkshire. Stone walls and barns grace the scenic fields of Yorkshire Dales.

Eurostar trains carry passengers under the English Channel from France all the way to Waterloo Station in London in just over two hours.

Did you know that England's currency is called the pound sterling? The pound is now worth one hundred pence, abbreviated p.

Channel Tunnel

In 1994 a tunnel was constructed beneath the English Channel, connecting France and England. The tunnel is called the Channel Tunnel and is nicknamed the Chunnel. Using the tunnel, a traveler can travel by train from Paris to London in just over two hours.

The red fox is found throughout England. Red foxes will eat anything they can lay their paws on. Many live close to cities and towns, as raccoons do in New York City.

Do you enjoy playing games in camp?

British children play some interesting games. They play cricket which is similar to baseball and rugby which is like American football. Dominoes are an all-time favorite in England.

Royal Pageantry

Pharaoh in Egypt wasn't the only one who celebrated his royal birthday! Cannon salutes are fired from the Tower of London on special days, such as the Queen's birthday. On these days the national anthem is traditionally played on BBC, the official British radio station, and a ceremony called Trooping the Colour is performed by regiments from the British armies.

Mounted bands of the Household Cavalry at Trooping the Colour. The rider of the black-and-white drum horse, working the reins with his feet, crosses drumsticks above his head in salute.

PLVS
VLTRA

Spain is the largest of the four countries on the Iberian Peninsula. A peninsula is a land area mostly surrounded by water. The Iberian Peninsula also contains Portugal, Gibraltar, and Andorra. The rest of the peninsula is bordered by the sea.

SPAIN

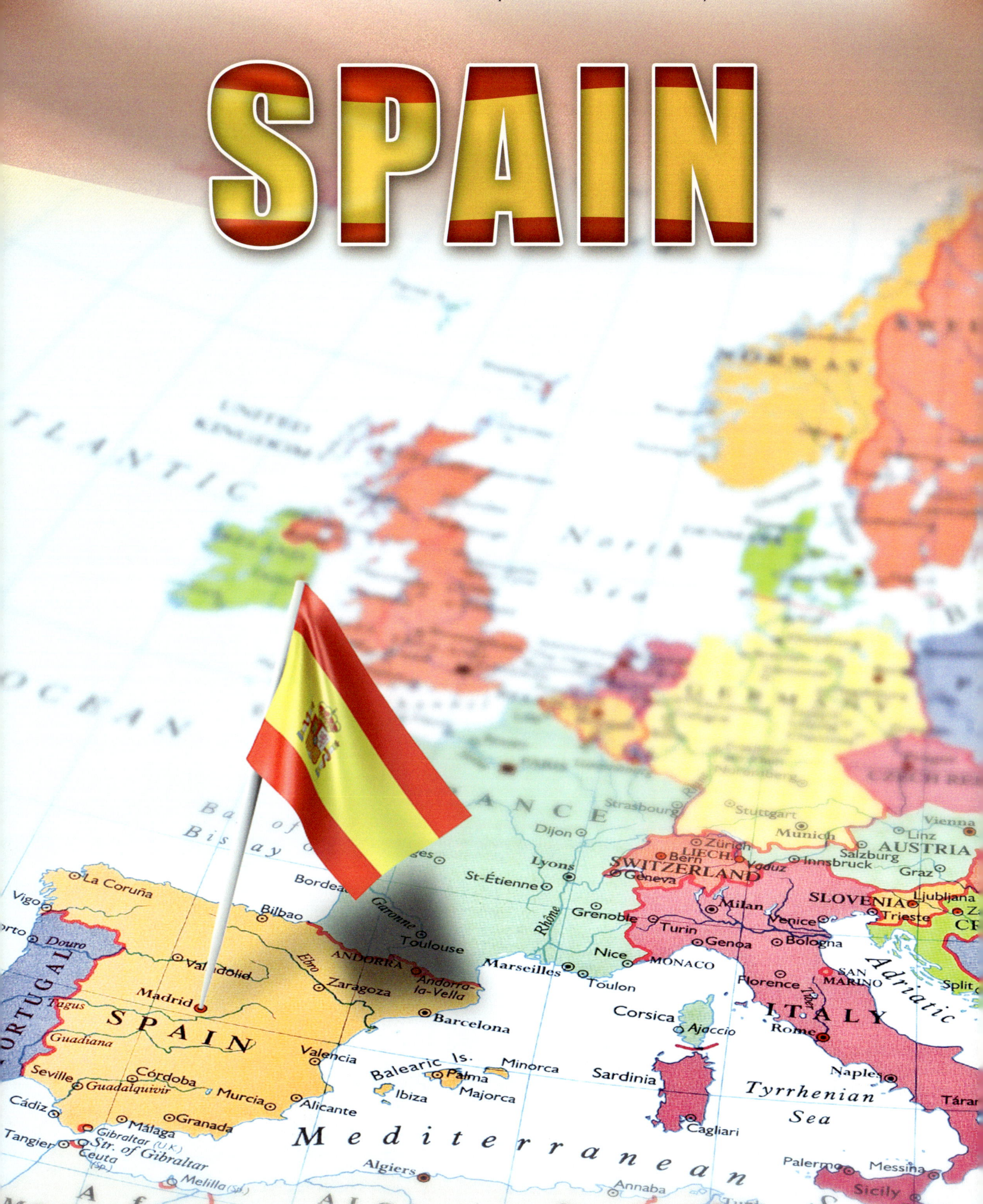

The History of the Jews in Spain

Jews have lived in Spain since the days of the Roman Empire. When the Romans conquered Yerushalayim, Emperor Vespasian sent some Jewish prisoners to Spain. Later, after the *Beis HaMikdash* was destroyed, thousands of Jews were taken there.

Life for the early Jews of Spain was generally peaceful. But as Spain became more and more Christian, things got worse. Jews were sometimes forced to become Christians. Other times they were thrown out of their homes in Spain. In the year 711 a dramatic change occurred. The Moors, who were Muslims from North Africa, conquered Spain. From the year 711 until the twelfth century, Spanish Jews enjoyed prosperity and power. This became known as the Golden Age of Spanish Jewry. At this time, many famous Jewish poets wrote *piyutim* — poems that speak of their love and longing for Hashem, their love of Eretz Yisrael and the love Hashem has for the Jewish nation.

Jews were also active in such fields as astronomy — the study of the sun, moon, stars, planets — medicine, and mathematics. They studied the natural world so that they could learn more about the work of Hashem and become closer to Him.

The Ramban

In Spain during the Middle Ages public debates were very popular. The kings would order Jewish rabbis to debate or argue with Christians about Judaism. Some of these so-called Christians were really Jews who had converted to Christianity.

By order of King James the First of Aragon, Spain, Rabbi Moshe ben Nachman, the *Ramban,* was forced to take part in a public debate against a Jewish convert in the King's presence. The Ramban gave a brilliant defense of Judaism and shamed the Christian convert. Because his victory was such an insult to the King's religion, the Ramban was forced to run away from Spain. He came to Yerushalayim where he found just a handful of Jewish families living in terrible poverty. He worked hard to rebuild the community and he built a shul in the Old City of Yerushalayim. That shul is in use today, more than eight hundred years later.

Beis Knesses HaRamban, in the Old City of Yerushalayim

After much fighting between the Muslims and the Christians, the Christians regained control of Spain in the 1200s. For the next two hundred years the Jews became more and more wealthy and powerful. They served as advisors to the king, bankers, scientists, doctors, traders, and scholars. Great *talmidei chachamim* such as Don Yitzchak Abarbanel became advisors to the king and his nobles. Jews became very wealthy and admired. This success caused many Christians to become jealous of the Jews. Christian clergymen were furious that the Jews had such power. The fact that so many Jews held such high positions in the king's palace actually set the stage for one of the darkest and most painful events in our long history.

In the 1400's horrible times began for the Jews. Cruel monks began to do terrible things to Jews who would not accept the Christian faith. Many Jews chose to die *al Kiddush Hashem,* but others did not have the strength to do so. They became Christians on the outside while many continued to do *mitzvos* in secret. The Christians called them "Marranos," which means "pigs," or "conversos" because they only pretended to convert.

These Jews built secret cellars where they would light Shabbos candles, make *Kiddush*, and even conduct the Pesach *Seder*. The heads of the church began to watch them. The church created a secret court called the Inquisition. Suspected conversos were tortured to force them to admit that they were loyal Jews. Then they were burned alive publicly, in order to strike terror into the hearts of the other conversos.

When we think of the Spanish Inquisition, we are filled with horror. We imagine the auto-da-fé where Jews were burnt at the stake in a public square, saying their last *Shema*, while the merciless, wicked mob of Christians cheered wildly. Many times terrified conversos would be sitting in the audience, watching with horror as their Jewish brothers were killed.

Finally, on Tishah B'Av in the year 1492, the Jews of Spain were driven out of the country by King Ferdinand and Queen Isabella. The Spanish Jews went to different parts of the world, including Holland, Morocco, Turkey, Algeria, France, and Italy. At least 200,000 Jews fled the country. About 20,000 of these Jews died on the journey. Some say that about 50,000 Jews remained in Spain, either converting or pretending to convert to Christianity. The Jews who had lived in Spain and then left it are called Sephardim.

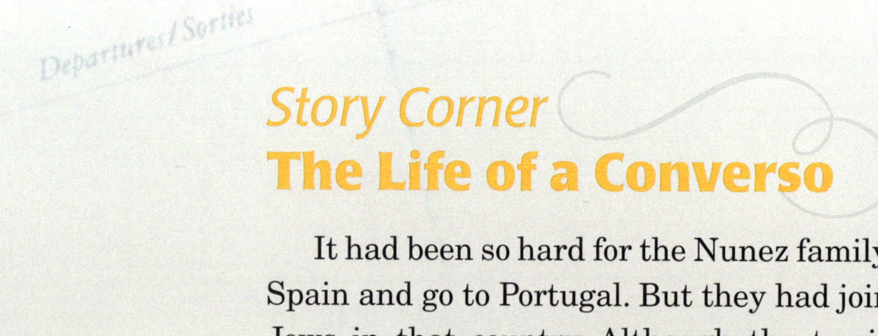

Story Corner

The Life of a Converso

It had been so hard for the Nunez family to leave their home in Spain and go to Portugal. But they had joined thousands of other Jews in that country. Although the terrifying Inquisition soon came to Portugal as well, the Nunez family continuted to observe the Torah in secret, avoiding detection for nearly 200 years.

Over time, the Nunez family developed close relations with government officials. In fact, Dr. Samuel (Diogo) Nunez had become the doctor of the King of Portugal. Dr. Nunez was wealthy and very popular with the nobility.

The Inquisition discovered that Dr. Nunez was secretly keeping *mitzvos* and practicing *Yiddishkeit*. They began to spy on him. Dr. Nunez realized that his days in Portugal were numbered. He came up with a daring plan.

He made a lavish banquet and invited many of his wealthy friends. During the banquet he announced a surprise in honor of his guests. He would give them a ride on his new, beautiful yacht. An hour or so after they boarded the yacht the guests suddenly realized that they were moving very quickly. In fact, they were sailing away from the shores of Portugal, heading for the "friendlier" shores of England — friendlier, that is, for the Nunez family! Dr. Nunez reassured his guests that as soon as they reached the shores of England, the boat would immediately turn around and return the guests to their homes. He apologized for the inconvenience. Eventually his family made their way to America.

The Abarbanel

In Spain some of the greatest Torah scholars were wealthy and powerful people. They were involved in business and politics, and served as royal bankers and statesman. **Don Yitzchak Abarbanel** is one of the great commentators on the Torah. His *peirush*, known as the Abarbanel, is still studied today. At the same time, he was a Jewish statesman who played an important part in Jewish history.

While Don Yitzchak (the Spanish title "Don" was used for the nobility and important people) was writing his *peirush* on *Sefer Melachim*, the King of Spain, King Ferdinand, summoned him to become the official treasurer of the king and queen. That very same year a bloodthirsty and cruel Christian friar, Tomas de Torquemada, became head of the Inquisition in Spain. Two years later, in the year 1492, the wicked Torquemada succeeded in convincing King Ferdinand and Queen Isabella to expel all the Jews from Spain. You can imagine how hard it was for families who had lived in Spain for hundreds of years to leave their country, their beautiful homes and gardens, their beloved shuls and treasured memories. This had always been the plight of the Jews for over two thousand years, since the *Beis HaMikdash* was destroyed. They were persecuted and exiled from one country to another.

When the terrible decree became known, Don Yitzchak Abarbanel begged the king and queen to reconsider. He offered a huge sum of money from his own fortune to the king's treasury. The king and queen were actually considering this, but Torquemada persuaded them not to.

Ferdinand offered to let Don Yitzchak Abarbanel stay in Spain and keep his important position, if only he would convert to Christianity. Of course the Abarbanel refused. On Tishah B'Av 1492, he gave up his powerful position and joined his people in exile and suffering. He later settled in Naples and Venice where many Spanish Jews resettled.

The Most Treasured Day

The most treasured day of the Jewish calendar for the Marranos in Spain and Portugal was Ta'anis Esther. Esther was the heroine of Spanish Jewry. Queen Esther had to keep the fact that she was a Jew a secret from everyone. The conversos, too, had to keep their faith in Torah and *Yiddishkeit* a deep secret.

The image of beautiful Esther, who had fasted for three days before going before King Achashveirosh, standing before the king for the sake of Hashem and her people, gave them strength. They too, stood before the Church, ready to give up their lives for the sake of Hashem.

Today most of us are lucky and live in places where we can openly practice our religion. We too, however, can look back at our rich heritage for strength and inspiration.

What's the Weather Like?

Spain is actually Europe's sunniest country, but in the northwest of Spain it rains frequently all year. The capital, Madrid, has an extreme climate. Summer temperatures above 105°F are common, while in the winter the weather could fall below freezing.

Did you know that Spain's coastlines run over three thousand miles along the Mediterranean Sea and Atlantic Ocean?

The waters of the Mediterranean are warmer than the Atlantic. Both oceans have a wide variety of marine life such as whales and dolphins.

Spain's Wildlife

A spotted Iberian lynx creeps quietly through the sand and the bushes. Its yellow eyes glinting, it prowls through Donana National Park in search of prey. The Iberian lynx is one of the most endangered animals in Europe. Spain has a wider variety of plants and animals than any other European country.

Iberian lynx

Donana National Park

The Canary Islands

The Canary Islands, which lie off the coast of Morocco, really belong to Spain. These islands form an archipelago, which is a large chain of islands. This archipelago has seven islands and many islets — tiny islands. It is named Canary Islands after the songbirds that come from these islands. Scientists are watching one of these islands, La Palma, very carefully. La Palma has a volcano that could cause a tsunami, a huge ocean wave caused by an underwater earthquake or an erupting volcano. This tsunami would be devastating for the eastern seaboard of the United States.

May Hashem protect us from such a disaster.

La Palma

Do You Like Chocolate?

Chocolate, one of our favorite snacks, is made from cacao beans. The credit for bringing chocolate to Europe is given to the Spanish conqueror of Mexico, Hernando Cortés. Cortés, who loved money, was very impressed because the Aztecs, local Indians, used cacao beans as money. For 100 cacao beans, a person could buy a slave. Cortés returned to Spain with the cacao beans and presented them to the king. Spain was the first country in Europe where "hot cacao" — hot chocolate — became a favorite drink. At first only noblemen could afford to buy it, but then it spread even to the common folk.

Spain is a Bull Market

Bulls are an important part of Spanish life. The most famous activity in Spain is bullfighting. It is considered a glorious battle between the enormous strength of the angry bull and the skill and speed of the matador, the bullfighter. A red cape is waved in front of the bull, enraging it. The matador neatly sidesteps the charging bull. Every once in a while a matador is killed but this is considered a worthwhile price to pay for such fun. Such a cruel sport is entirely understandable for people whose ancestors used to watch and cheer when Jewish conversos were burnt at the stake.

Information Corner

The official language of Spain is Spanish.

Some common Spanish phrases that you may be familiar with are:

buenas dias (good morning)

buenas noches (good evening)

por favor (please)

gracias (thank you)

Ner Shabbos, Ner Chanukah

If you travel through Andalusia in Spain you will see miles and miles of olive groves with thousands of trees. Spain is the world's largest producer of olive oil. It produces about 45 percent of the world's total olive oil production. Much of the olive oil we use for Shabbos, and Yom Tov, and Chanukah *neiros* comes from Spain.

Seeks the Welfare of His Nation

Over a thousand years ago a great Jewish scholar and statesman by the name of **Chasdai ibn Shaprut** lived in Spain. Because of his great wealth, wisdom, and power, Chasdai was in a position to help his fellow Jews, much like Mordechai in Shushan. He was the *Nassi*, or head, of all the Jews in Spain. He was very wealthy and tried to help the Jews in business. At the same time, he was a great *talmid chacham.* He built yeshivos and wrote to the Gaonim of Bavel. He surrounded himself with many famous scholars and *paytanim,* who wrote poetic *tefillos*. Among them are Menachem ibn Saruk and Dunash ibn Labrat, both quoted by Rashi. It was during his time that Spain's Golden Era began.

The Rambam

The Rambam, **Rabbi Moshe Ben Maimon**, was born Erev Pesach in the year 1135 in Cordoba, Spain. He was a descendant of Rabbi Yehudah HaNassi, who compiled the Mishnah, and farther back, hailed from *Malchus Beis David*, the royal house of David HaMelech. His father, Rabbi Maimon, was his first Rebbe and taught him Tanach, Talmud, and every aspect of Torah and *Yiddishkeit*. He also taught him science.

Moshe was barely bar mitzvah when a group of wild and pitiless Muslims conquered Cordoba. For the next ten years, Moshe's family wandered from one Spanish city to another.

They traveled to Morocco and about five years later, by way of Yerushalayim, made their way to Egypt. Even though they were on the run, Reb Moshe continued to learn Torah constantly.

In Yerushalayim the family davened near the site of th Beis HaMikdash, and in Chevron, at the Me'aras HaMachpeilah, where the *Avos* are buried. From there they proceeded to Egypt.

In Egypt, the Maimon family went through a very difficult time. First Rav Maimon died. Then the Rambam's brother David, who was supporting the whole family, died very suddenly. He was a gem merchant and had gone on a business trip to India. The ship David was sailing on was shipwrecked in the Indian Ocean and David drowned. To make things even worse, the family's entire fortune went down with the ship as well. To support the family, Rav Moshe, with his vast knowledge of medicine, worked as a doctor, since he did not want to be paid for his vast Torah knowledge. He only wanted to learn Torah *lishmah*, for the sake of Hashem. He was such a successful doctor that he became the court physician of the ruler of Egypt, the Sultan Saladin himself.

Despite his incredibly busy schedule, Rambam became known as the greatest Talmudic scholar. Jews from all over the world sent him questions.

The Rambam wrote some of the most important *sefarim* we have on Torah, Halachah, and Jewish philosophy. Some of the most widely used of his *sefarim* are *Mishneh Torah, Peirush HaMishnah*, and *Sefer HaMitzvos*.

The kever of the Rambam, R' Moshe ben Maimon.

France is the largest country in Western Europe. It is almost as big as the state of Texas. It shares borders with Italy, Switzerland, Germany, Luxemburg, Belgium, and Spain. France also borders the Atlantic Ocean, the English Channel, and the Mediterranean Sea.

FRANCE

The History of the Jews in France

After the Second *Beis HaMikdash* was destroyed, boatloads of Jewish captives were brought to the area that would become known as France. This was the beginning of what would later be one of the largest Jewish communities in Europe.

Throughout the Middle Ages, up until the 1700's, life in France was very hard for the Jews. Sometimes whole Jewish communities were forced to leave their homes, or were even murdered in cold blood. There were also blood libels, where Jews were accused of killing Christian children to use their blood. Despite these hardships, Torah learning thrived in the Middle Ages. Rashi, Rabbeinu Tam, some of the Baalei Tosafos, and many other Torah sages lived in France during this time.

In 1799 Napoleon Bonaparte became the ruler of France. Napoleon made the Jews full citizens and gave them civil rights. He appointed a "Sanhedrin" of seventy-one rabbis and others to establish rules that wold be binding on all Jews.

By the late 1800's Jews had become very active in many areas of French life. The Jewish community prospered, but anti-Semitism was far from over. In 1894 Captain Alfred Dreyfus, a French Jew and a well-known member of the French army, was arrested. The army claimed he was a traitor. He was sentenced to life imprisonment on Devil's Island, a horrible prison. His arrest shocked the Jews of France, because it was clear that Dreyfus was innocent. Years later, it was shown that high-ranking army officers had lied at his trial. Captain Dreyfus was eventually pardoned and actually rejoined the French army.

In 1940, when the Nazis invaded France, there were about 350,000 Jews living in France. Over the course of the war, 75,000 French Jews had been killed.

Devil's Island

After the war, Jewish refugees poured into France. Later, many Sephardim came from the Arab countries of North Africa. Today there are between 500,000 and 600,000 Jews in France. Half of them live in Paris. More than half of the Jews of France are Sephardic.

Today, there are six million Muslims living in France. The country is developing close ties to the Arab world. Many French Jews are afraid of Islamic terrorism, which seems to be on the rise in France. About 3,000 French Jews make *aliyah* — move to Eretz Yisrael — every year, and the number is growing. Still, France remains Europe's largest Jewish community.

Unfortunately, many French Jews are unaware of their rich Jewish heritage. In the United States, although there are many centers of Torah and *Yiddishkeit* in places like New York and Lakewood, the percentage of *frum* Yidden is even lower than in France. We eagerly await the day when Hashem will gather all of the exiles and we will all live in Eretz Yisrael, basking in Hashem's holy Shechinah and visiting the newly-rebuilt *Beis HaMikdash*. We daven that one day this book will be read by generations of Jewish children who will never know of exile, suffering, or death.

Visas Departures / Sorties Entrées

Do you remember how happy you were when you began learning Rashi? Starting to learn Rashi is like beginning a wonderful journey that will last a lifetime.

The name "Rashi" stands for **Rabbi Shlomo Yitzchaki**. "Yitzchaki" means that Rashi's father's name was Yitzchak.

Rashi was born in France about 900 years ago, in the town of Troyes. He was a descendant of David HaMelech.

When Rashi was still young he left his home and went to study under great Torah sages. After eight years of learning day and night, he returned to Troyes. He became known as a brilliant scholar and many students came to learn from him.

Rashi wrote his famous *peirush*, commentary, in simple language that would make it easy for everyone to learn and understand Torah. There is a legend that says that Rashi wanted to see if his *peirush* would be helpful. Without telling anyone who he was, he traveled around France and put slips of papers with his *peirush* in different yeshivos. When Rashi saw how much everyone liked what he'd written he continued writing his commentary on the entire *Chumash*, *Neviim*, and most of the Talmud.

After a while the secret came out and people realized who had written this wonderful *peirush*. Rashi's name became known throughout the world. Rashi's commentary is still studied today, in every yeshivah and by every Jew who learns Torah, young and old. The study of Torah and Talmud is unthinkable without Rashi.

The next time your beloved Rebbe says *"zugt der heilige Rashi* — the holy Rashi says," you will know that Rashi was a gift that *HaKadosh Baruch Hu* gave his beloved nation nearly a thousand years ago. Rashi continues to open up our eyes to the vast treasures of the Torah to this very day.

Children throughout the generations learning Chumash with Rashi

Rashi was one of the greatest Torah sages to come from France. Another great French scholar was Rashi's grandson, **Rabbeinu Yaakov ben Meir Tam**, who is known as Rabbeinu Tam.

Rabbeinu Tam was born in the French city of Ramerupt. Rashi had no sons, and Rabbeinu Tam's mother was Yocheved, one of Rashi's daughters. Rabbeinu Tam's father, Rabbi Meir, was a *talmid chacham*, and he taught his son Torah. Another of Rabbeinu Tam's teachers was his older brother, the famous Rashbam.

Rabbeinu Tam became the head of a great yeshivah. At one time his yeshivah included 80 scholars who came to be known as the *Baalei Tosafos*. Their teachings were compiled into a famous *peirush* on the Talmud called Tosafos. It appears on almost every page of Gemara.

You may have heard of Rabbeinu Tam tefillin. They are a little different from the regular tefillin, which are called Rashi tefillin. Everyone wears Rashi tefillin, but some people wear both types. They wear Rashi tefillin during davening, and put on Rabbeinu Tam tefillin at the end of davening. You may want to ask your father and grandfather if they put on Rabbeinu Tam tefillin.

A Narrow Escape

Rabbeinu Tam narrowly escaped from death. On the second day of Shavuos, a group of Crusaders, violent Christians who wanted to force everyone to accept their religion, rode into the town where Rabbeinu Tam lived and killed many Jews. Rabbeinu Tam was a rich man, so they broke into his house and stole all his money. They wounded Rabbeinu Tam and were about to kill him, but Hashem protected him miraculously, and he was saved at the last minute by a wealthy nobleman.

Rashi Shul in Worms, Germany

Photo by photos8.com

The Burning of the Talmud

9 Tammuz 5002 (1242). Terrifying screams echoed through the streets of Paris. "Bring the Jewish books!" shouted the mob. Over twenty wagons filled with about 12,000 handwritten manuscripts of the Talmud were taken by wooden carts to a large square in Paris, on the River Seine. Remember, this was before the printing press had been invented. It had taken scribes weeks, months, even years of work to write every one of the precious manuscripts.

A gigantic fire had been set in the public square. Priests and other important officials held front-row seats. Royal guards lifted the holy *sefarim* from the wagons and threw them into the flames.

How did such a terrible act happen? It began with a debate between Christian scholars and Jewish rabbis. The rabbis, of course, did not want to argue about religion with the priests, but they were forced to.

Sadly, the person representing the Christians was a *meshumad* — a Jew who had left his *Yiddishkeit* and joined another religion. His name was Nicholas Donin. He debated four of the leading Rabbanim of that time, led by one of the Baalei Tosafos, Rabbenu Yechiel of Paris. Although Donin did not argue successfully and he was not able to prove anything against the Jews, the judges, who were all Christian, ruled that the Talmud should be burned. The Jews were shocked. They had never imagined that the church would commit such an act. Such a thing had never happened before. The terrible act took place on Friday. You can imagine how sad the Jews were and how difficult it must have been to prepare for Shabbos that week.

A *Sefer Torah* or Talmud is the most precious thing we have. If a Jew sees a Torah burned, he has to tear *kriyah* on his clothing, which is usually done only when a close relative dies.

Paris is nicknamed The City of Light, but on that Erev Shabbos, Paris was lit up by the flames of anti-Semitism and evil. The terrible pain of that day was never forgotten. Every Tishah B'Av we say the *kinnah "Shaali Srufah Ba'aish,"* which was written by the Maharam of Rottenberg about this terrible decree.

L'chaim!

The French city of Bordeaux is famous for its wine. More than 13,000 grape growers live there. Next time your father makes *Kiddush*, look at the wine bottle. The wine may have been made in Bordeaux, France.

Crossing the Alps

While France has several mountain ranges, the Alps, with many high peaks, are the country's most famous mountains. Europe's highest mountain, Mont Blanc, rises out of the French Alps at a height of 15,771 feet above sea level.

Did you know that the Rhine River in France empties into the Mediterranean Sea?

The area just east of the Rhine is called the French Riviera, where many enjoy the warm waters and beautiful weather.

Can you imagine?

When Marie Antoinette, the last queen of France, was told that her subjects were starving and had no bread she haughtily and famously replied, "Let them eat cake." Sounds like a page out of Vashti's royal book!

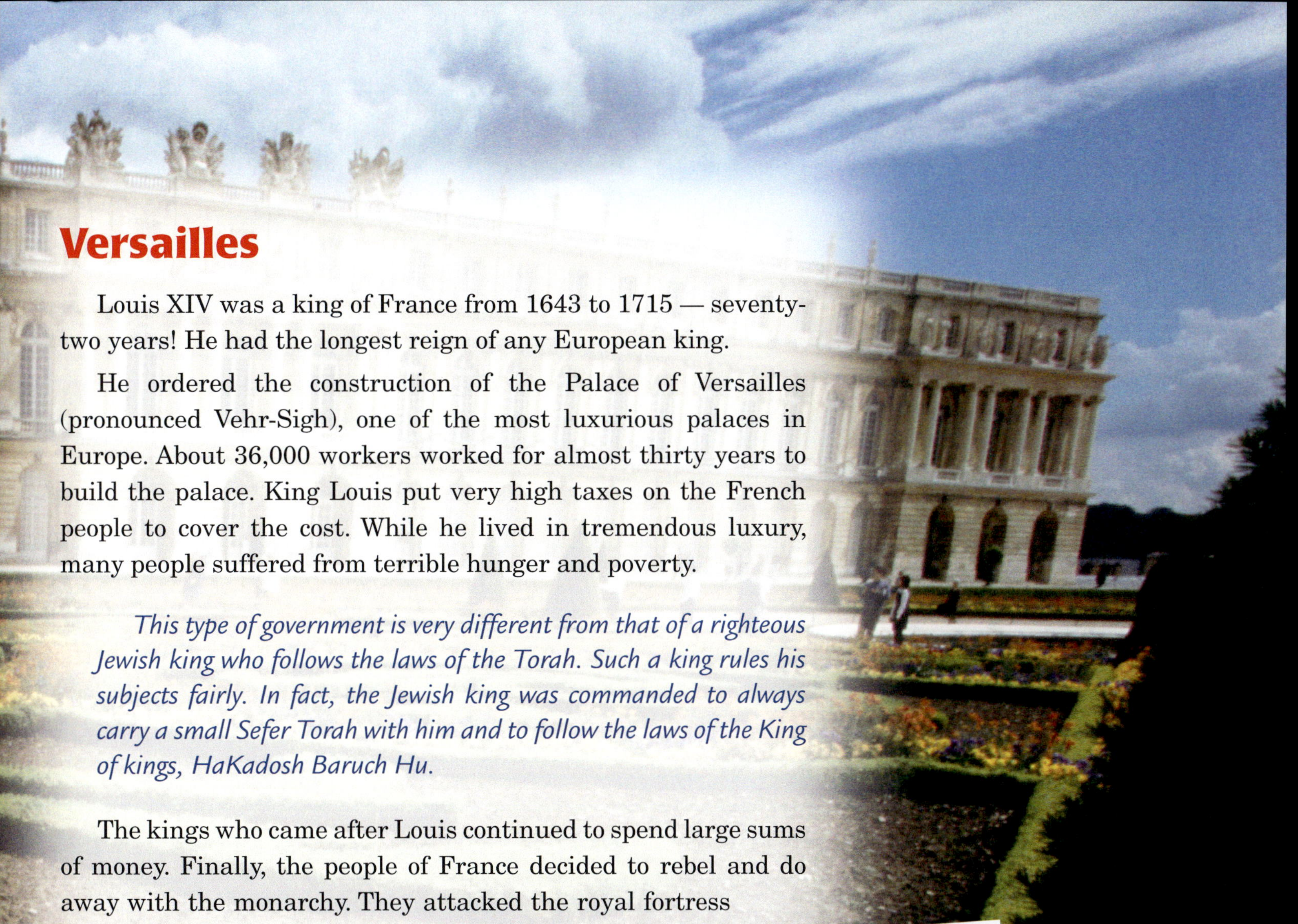

Versailles

Louis XIV was a king of France from 1643 to 1715 — seventy-two years! He had the longest reign of any European king.

He ordered the construction of the Palace of Versailles (pronounced Vehr-Sigh), one of the most luxurious palaces in Europe. About 36,000 workers worked for almost thirty years to build the palace. King Louis put very high taxes on the French people to cover the cost. While he lived in tremendous luxury, many people suffered from terrible hunger and poverty.

This type of government is very different from that of a righteous Jewish king who follows the laws of the Torah. Such a king rules his subjects fairly. In fact, the Jewish king was commanded to always carry a small Sefer Torah with him and to follow the laws of the King of kings, HaKadosh Baruch Hu.

The kings who came after Louis continued to spend large sums of money. Finally, the people of France decided to rebel and do away with the monarchy. They attacked the royal fortress called the Bastille in 1789. They fought for 10 years and then declared France a republic.

A statue in Versaille depicting King Louis XIV

Sad But True ...

Many French Jews were very grateful to Napoleon for giving them freedom, but many *gedolim* were not so enthusiastic. Napoleon gave the Jews permission to leave the ghettos as they pleased. He threw open the walls of the ghetto and allowed Jews to mix with Western European society. While it is true that life became much easier for the Jews, this freedom also brought terrible problems. Yidden began mixing with the non-Jews. They attended their universities, worked alongside them, and mingled with them in every way. This led to much weakening of *Yiddishkeit* for some Jews. Unfortunately some Yidden became totally assimilated and even intermarried with non-Jews, leaving *Yiddishkeit* forever.

Napoleon Visits a Shul

Many stories are told about Napoleon, the famous French general who took control of the country in 1799. One of these stories actually took place in a shul!

Napoleon happened to enter a shul somewhere in Europe on the night of Tishah B'Av. Of course the Jews were sitting on the floor or on low stools. The *ba'al korei* read *Eichah* in the customary sad tune, and many people were crying.

"What happened? Why is everybody weeping?" Napoleon asked.

The Jews explained that they were mourning the destruction of their Temple, which had been destroyed almost two thousand years before. Hearing these words, Napoleon wisely said, "If the Jewish nation is still mourning something that happened two thousand years ago, they will never be destroyed. They will forever remain the Jewish nation." And he was absolutely right!

One of the many beautiful shuls found throughout Europe.

Photo courtesy of Joel and Linda Berkowitz

Rothschild & Sons

One family that, tragically, lost much of their connection to *Yiddishkeit* was the famous Rothschild family. The founder of the great banking family, Meir Amschel Rothschild, was a religious Jew who gave much *tzedakah* and learned Torah. His children became fabulously wealthy and were friends with many of Europe's non-Jewish aristocracy. Sadly, many of his grandchildren and great-grandchildren married non-Jews. Today nearly all of the original Rothschild family is totally assimilated. While they are still very powerful and wealthy, they were robbed of their greatest treasure, the Holy Torah.

The Rothschild coat of arms

Story Corner

The Sun and the Wind

Once upon a time a man stood in an open field. The sun and the wind began arguing about who was more powerful. They decided to make a test, to see who would be able to take the man's coat off, proving who was the more powerful of the two. The wind was first to try. He blew furiously around the man, nearly lifting him off the ground. Stubbornly the man wrapped himself even more tightly in his coat, holding it closely around him. The wind finally calmed down and admitted defeat.

Now the sun came out in all her radiant glory. She shone down on the man, warming him with her rays. The man became very, very hot. Slowly, he began to open his coat. He took his arms out of the sleeves, and finally he removed the coat altogether.

This *mashal* shows us that sometimes when Esav acts warmly to Yaakov, like a brother, the damage he does with his friendship is far greater than when he is a cold and windy enemy!

Arc de Triomphe

The Arc de Triomphe is one of the most famous monuments in Paris. It sits at the meeting point of 12 grand avenues. It was built in the early 1800's and it honors those who fought for France, particularly in the revolution and during Napoleon's time.

The Louvre

Located in Paris, the Louvre is one of the largest museums in the world. It is also one of the oldest museums, having been opened to the public in 1793. The famous collections of the Louvre grew from the works of art bought by the kings of France for their own enjoyment. Ruler after ruler added more treasures. The Louvre is now a national, or state-owned, museum.

The Eiffel Tower

The Eiffel Tower was designed and built by Gustave Eiffel to be used as an entrance arch to the 1899 World's Fair, which was held in Paris. Some artists thought it was ugly, and it was almost pulled down 20 years after the exhibition. Today it is considered an icon, which means a symbol, of Paris.

It is 984 feet high and the view of Paris from the top is spectacular.

The view from the top of the Eiffel Tower

INVASION!

The Second World War had been raging for years. Much of France was under German rule. On June 6, 1944, famously known as D-Day, thousands of Allied troops landed on the beaches of Normandy, France. They swiftly moved across France, freeing people from German troops. After this, the war went very badly for the Germans. Finally, the German leader, Adolph Hitler *ym'sh*, killed himself on April 30, 1945. He had murdered six million Jews in 6 years.

May Hashem avenge the blood of our brothers and sisters, who will never be forgotten.

U.S. Troops wading through water amid Nazi gunfire

Yiddish, the "Mamma Loshen"

A wise person once observed, "If you can speak three languages, you are trilingual. If you can speak two languages you are bilingual. If you can speak only one language you are an American." Of course, many *frum* American Jews speak some Hebrew and others speak Yiddish, but in Europe many Ashkenazi children speak three languages, including Yiddish, quite fluently.

Yiddish is called by many the "Mamma Loshen" — the mother tongue. Some feel that centuries of Jews speaking and learning in Yiddish has inbued the language with a degree of *kedushah*. Yiddish developed and adjusted and changed, just like the Jews who had to constantly adjust to exile and suffering. The Western European Yiddish sounded different from that of Eastern Europe. Still, Yiddish was and remains today a unifying point of connection for all Ashkenazic Jews. Yiddish has a special flavor; it is really "*geshmak*!"

ITALY

OCEAN
Bay of Biscay
Gironde
Limoges
Lyons
St-Étienne
Bordeaux
Garonne
Toulouse
Grenoble
Rhône
Nice
Marseilles
Toulon
MONACO
Turin
Genoa
Milan
Bologna
Florence
SAN MARINO
ITALY
Rome
Adriatic
Split
SLOVENIA
Ljubljana
Trieste
AUSTRIA
Salzburg
Innsbruck
Graz
Linz
La Coruña
Vigo
Bilbao
Douro
PORTUGAL
Valladolid
Ebro
ANDORRA
Andorra-la-Vella
Zaragoza
Madrid
Tagus
SPAIN
Barcelona
Guadiana
Valencia
Balearic Is.
Minorca
Palma
Majorca
Ibiza
Seville
Córdoba
Guadalquivir
Murcia
Alicante
Cádiz
Málaga
Granada
Gibraltar (U.K.)
Str. of Gibraltar
Tangier
Ceuta (Sp.)
Melilla (Sp.)
Corsica
Ajaccio
Sardinia
Cagliari
Naples
Tyrrhenian Sea
Mediterranean Sea
Algiers
Annaba
Tunis
Constantine
Palermo
Messina
Sicily
Catánia
Pantelleria
ALGERIA
MOROCCO

The History of the Jews in Italy

The first Jews in Italy settled there about 200 years before the *Churban*, the destruction of the Second *Beis HaMikdash*, during the time that the Maccabees ruled in Eretz Yisrael. These Jews lived in Rome. The Jewish community in Rome grew larger after the *Churban Bayis Sheini*, the destruction of the Second *Beis HaMikdash*.

Victory coins with the words: "Judea Capta" — Judea is captive.

After the *Churban*, a very large monument was built in Rome. It is called the Arch of Titus, and is named after the evil Roman general who burned down the *Beis HaMikdash*. This 51-foot monument was built to mark Titus' victories, including the capture of Jerusalem. Carved on the arch is an image of Titus in his chariot and a line of Jewish prisoners carrying the Shulchan, the Menorah, and the silver trumpets taken from the *Beis HaMikdash* by the Romans.

The Arch of Titus still stands. Many Jews will not walk under it because it symbolizes the Roman victory, the defeat of the Jews, and the destruction of the *Beis HaMikdash*.

The Romans were so overjoyed at having destroyed the *Beis HaMikdash* that they minted a special coin in honor of the occasion. On one side of the coin was a picture of a victorious Roman captor and on the other side was a Jewish woman crying for her loved ones.

Sculpted onto the Arch of Titus are images of Jewish prisoners carrying the Menorah and other vessels.

Targum Unkelos

Titus was the wicked Roman general who was sent to capture Yerushalayim. He broke through the city's walls and entered the Holy Temple. Our Sages tell us that Titus took his sword and stabbed the *Paroches*, the curtain that stood before the Holy of Holies. The *Paroches* actually began to bleed!

When he'd finished his awful deeds Titus took the *Paroches* and wrapped many beautiful and holy things that he'd stolen from the *Beis HaMikdash* in it. On the voyage home from Rome, a huge wave came to drown him. Arrogantly Titus called out "The Jewish G-d is only powerful on the sea. This is how he punished Pharoh as well. If He is truly mighty then I challenge Him to come to dry land and do battle with me."

A *bas kol*, a voice from the heavens, proclaimed "Wicked man, son of the wicked Eisav, I have a tiny creature in my world called a gnat. Come to dry land and do battle with her there."

Although Titus marched triumphantly into Rome, his glory did not last long. An insect flew into his nose and entered his brain. For seven years, the little insect hammered inside his head, causing him terrible suffering. After his death, they opened his head and found that the insect had grown to the size of a bird!

Right before he died Titus told his servants, "Burn my body and spread the ashes over the seven seas." He was foolish as well as evil, and he thought that this would help him escape Hashem's judgment.

Onkelos was Titus's nephew. After Titus's death Onkelos decided to convert and become a Jew. He somehow was able to contact Titus' soul. He asked him "What is important in the next world?" Titus answered, "Yisrael — the Jewish Nation." Onkelos then asked Titus if he should join the Jewish nation. Titus answered that he did not think that Onkelos would be able to keep all the *mitzvos*. Titus advised Onkelos to cause the Jews trouble, because all the arch-enemies of the Jews are important people. A simple person would be unworthy to fight with this great nation.

Onkelos asked Titus what kind of punishment he was receiving. He told Onkelos that his punishment was one that he had asked for himself. He had asked that his body be burned, so every day his ashes were collected and burned anew.

Instead of listening to his wicked uncle's advice, Onkelos did indeed become a *ger*, a convert. He wrote a translation of the *Chumash* that is used to this very day! It is found in almost every *Chumash*.

Caesar the Ger

Before Titus came to conquer Yerushalayim, another Roman Caesar, Nero, wanted to do the evil deed. But even the Roman Caesars knew that the Jewish G-d and His nation had to be reckoned with. Nero decided to find out whether or not Hashem would allow him to defeat the Jews.

Nero shot an arrow in all four directions of the compass. Each time the arrow somehow turned around toward Yerushalayim. He then met a Jewish boy. Nero asked him to tell him what he had learned that day. The boy quoted a *pasuk* that said that Hashem would take revenge against the Edomim, or Romans, for what they did to His nation.

When he heard this, Nero was overcome with fear and awe of Hashem. He left his position as ruler of Rome, ran away, and converted. Our sages tell us that the great Rabbi Meir comes from Nero the Convert!

The Coliseum

The Coliseum is a symbol of the cruelty of the Romans. It was an enormous stadium where slaves and gladiators would be forced to fight against ferocious wild animals. The Romans cheered enthusiastically as the animals tore their victims apart.

The Coliseum was built by Vespasian. He was a Roman general who was fighting in Eretz Yisrael. Not long before the *Beis HaMikdash* was destroyed, Vespasian was called to return to Rome to become emperor. Construction of the Coliseum began about the year 70. After Vespasian's death, it was finished by his son, Titus. It is said that the Coliseum was constructed using the money gained from the Roman victory over Judea (Eretz Yisrael).

Did you know

that after the destruction of the *Beis HaMikdash*, thousands of Jewish slaves were deported to Rome and forced to help build the Coliseum?

The Middle Ages

For three hundred years after the *Churban*, Jews settled in Italian towns such as Syracuse, Pompeii, Milan, and Otranto.

In the year 380, Christianity was recognized as the official religion of Italy. During the next thirteen hundred years, the Jews sometimes lived peaceful lives. At other times they faced great hatred and anti-Semitism, depending on the attitude of each Pope, the leader of the Catholic Church.

For many years during the Middle Ages, Jews were not allowed to take part in most businesses and professions. The only thing they were permitted to do was to become money lenders or to sell used clothing. Somehow, using their wits, the Jews managed to make a living, but it wasn't easy! Both noblemen who needed money to fight their wars and simple people who had to take loans borrowed from Jewish moneylenders. Shakespeare, the famous British playwright, ridiculed a Jewish moneylender named Shylock in one of his plays. Shylock has become a twisted symbol of Jewish greed that anti-Semites have pointed to throughout the generations.

The city of Milan, Italy

The First Ghetto Is Created

After the Spanish Expulsion of 1492, many Spanish Jews fled to Italy. Among them were many famous Spanish Jews, such as **Don Yitzchak Abarbanel**, who moved to Naples, Italy. Don Yitzchak Abarbanel and his sons had excellent relations with great ruling families of Italy and were the pride of Italian Jewry. They were soon joined in Italy by many Jews from Portugal after the Jews were expelled from that country.

In 1516 the first ghetto in Venice was established. Venice's Jewish neighborhood was the site of a cannon factory, and the word "ghetto" is actually the Italian word for "foundry," a factory where metal objects such as cannons are made.

Ghettos were areas where Jews were forced to live. The ghettos were very often dirty and small, with limited space, yet no Jew ever went without a roof over his head. Much of the Jewish character was forged in the ghetto.

The Modern World

In the 1800's much of Europe became freer. The laws keeping Jews in the ghettos were changed. In Italy some Jews began joining non-Jewish society and left their beautiful Jewish heritage. Others held onto their *mesorah,* traditions.

In 1940, Benito Mussolini, who called himself Il Duce (the leader), took Italy into World War II on Germany's side against the Allies. Though there were laws passed against the Jews, the Italians did not treat the Jews as badly as the Germans did. It was only when the Germans took over parts of Italy that the Jews were sent to death camps. In all, about 7,500 Italian Jews were murdered by Nazis.

In 1943 Allied troops landed in Sicily, a large island off the coast of Italy. From there they invaded Italy. Mussolini was ultimately thrown out of office by his own people and then captured and executed by Italian patriots.

May all our enemies meet a similar fate.

After the Holocaust many Italian Jews moved to Eretz Yisrael. Today, although there is a Jewish community in Italy, it is only a shadow of what it once was.

Did you know that the currency used in Italy is the euro, widely used in much of Europe?

Volcanos

What is a volcano? The inside of the earth is very, very hot. When there are deep cracks in the earth, sometimes the hot melted earth inside, called magma, flows out to the surface, where it is called "lava." The hot lava rock is not hard, but rather a thick liquid, like honey. When this happens, we say that the volcano is erupting. Once outside, the lava then becomes cold and hard, creating a hill or mountain. When a volcano erupts — watch out!

The Italian peninsula stands on a fault line, a deep crack on the Earth's surface. Because of this, there are many volcanoes and earthquakes.

Mount Vesuvius is a volcano located near Naples, Italy. Not long after the destruction of the Second *Beis HaMikdash*, in the year 79, one day after Tishah B'Av, Mount Vesuvius erupted. There was a huge explosion. Lava – liquid rocks — from the mountain rained down onto the city of Pompeii, and everyone who lived there was killed. Thousands of people died. It is interesting to note that Pompeii was a vacation spot, a sinful Roman city.

For almost 1700 years, Pompeii was buried under tons of ash from the volcano. People forgot it had ever existed. Then archeologists started to dig, and in 1748, they uncovered the buried city. They found houses, temples, and shops. Most things weren't broken at all, because the hot ash had kept them preserved and safe. They even unearthed a bakery with bread still in the oven and eggs with the shells still intact.

Did you know that no other country in Europe has as many volcanoes as Italy?

Did you know that the lava bursting forth from the rim of a volcano is about 1800°F?

Mt. Vesuvius

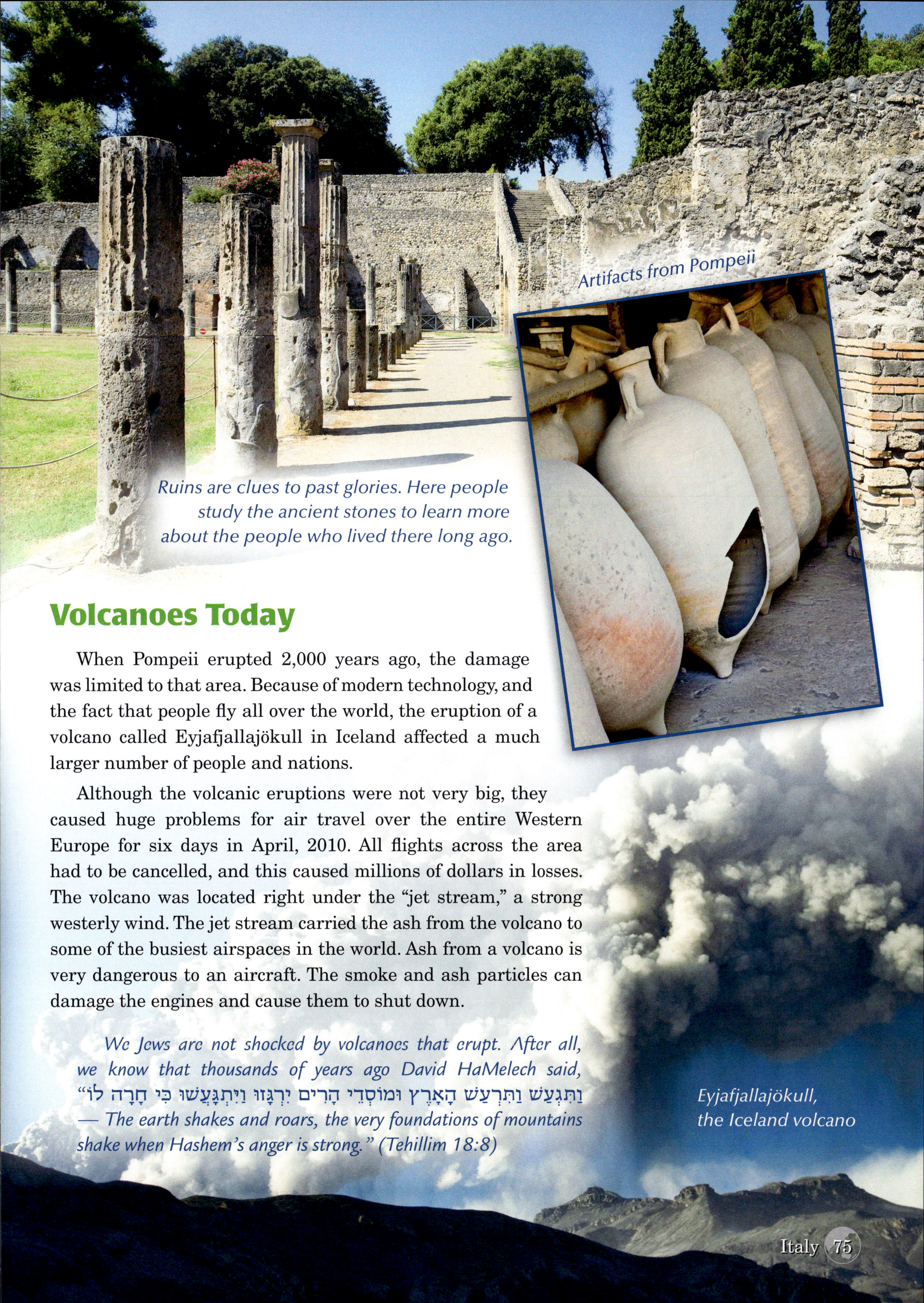

Artifacts from Pompeii

Ruins are clues to past glories. Here people study the ancient stones to learn more about the people who lived there long ago.

Volcanoes Today

When Pompeii erupted 2,000 years ago, the damage was limited to that area. Because of modern technology, and the fact that people fly all over the world, the eruption of a volcano called Eyjafjallajökull in Iceland affected a much larger number of people and nations.

Although the volcanic eruptions were not very big, they caused huge problems for air travel over the entire Western Europe for six days in April, 2010. All flights across the area had to be cancelled, and this caused millions of dollars in losses. The volcano was located right under the "jet stream," a strong westerly wind. The jet stream carried the ash from the volcano to some of the busiest airspaces in the world. Ash from a volcano is very dangerous to an aircraft. The smoke and ash particles can damage the engines and cause them to shut down.

We Jews are not shocked by volcanoes that erupt. After all, we know that thousands of years ago David HaMelech said, "וַתִּגְעַשׁ וַתִּרְעַשׁ הָאָרֶץ וּמוֹסְדֵי הָרִים יִרְגָּזוּ וַיִּתְגָּעֲשׁוּ כִּי חָרָה לוֹ — The earth shakes and roars, the very foundations of mountains shake when Hashem's anger is strong." (Tehillim 18:8)

Eyjafjallajökull, the Iceland volcano

Venice

Venice is one of the world's most beautiful and unusual cities. Its palaces and elegant homes do not stand on regular streets, but rather along canals. Many people move around by vaporetti, or water buses. The city was founded on a collection of muddy islands in a wide shallow lagoon. Hundreds of thousands of tourists visit the city every year. Perhaps one day you will ride on a small boat called a gondola, guided by a gondolier. Venice is currently under threat. It has been sinking into the mud for centuries. In addition, rising sea levels have caused frequent floods.

Do you wear glasses? *Did you know* that in the 14th century, eyeglasses were already being produced in Venice?

We would indeed have a dim view of life without our eyeglasses.

"Hey, taxi!"

The Grand Canal in Venice at sunset

The World's Greatest Violins

Stradivarius violins are regarded as the finest violins ever crafted. They were made by an Italian named Stradivari in the early 1700's. They are still played and prized by professional violinists today. In June 2011, a 1721 Stradivarius violin was bought for 15 million dollars, with all the money going to help the victims of a Japanese earthquake. Usually Stradivarius violins sell for about three million dollars.

Tempio Maggiore in Rome, Italy

The interior of the shul in Casale Monfaratto, Italy

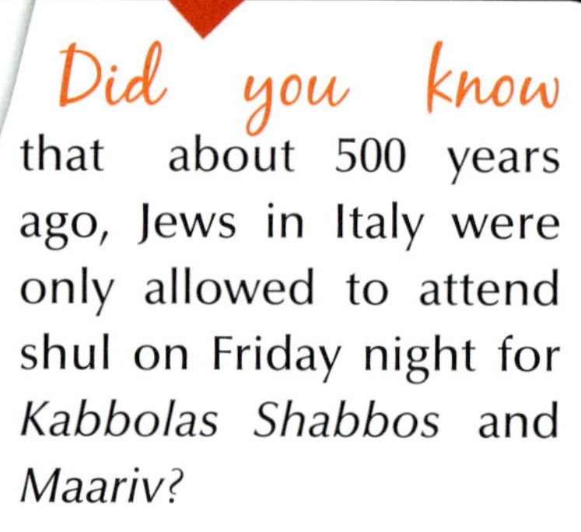

Did you know that about 500 years ago, Jews in Italy were only allowed to attend shul on Friday night for *Kabbolas Shabbos* and *Maariv?*

On Shabbos day they were marched from a central square to four different churches, where they were forced to listen to religious speeches. In order to avoid hearing these Christian sermons, the Jews stuffed up their ears to muffle the sounds.

Shuls of the Past

The Italians were extremely skilled and talented artisans who built the most magnificent shuls. Close your eyes and imagine hundreds of Jews davening in one of the gorgeous shuls, with a gold-covered *aron kodesh,* Jewish images on the walls and stained glass windows designed by creative and talented artists. Many of these breathtakingly magnificent shuls stand empty today. You can hear your voice echoing beneath the high ceiling, joining with the memory of past *tefillos* offered by Jews of a time long since gone. Although some of these shuls davened *Nusach Ashkenaz,* and some *Nusach Sefard,* many davened *"Nusach Italian,"* an ancient version of *tefillah* that hailed from the era of the Geonim of Italy.

Transplanted Shuls

After World War II, Italian Jews were responsible for the transfer of forty shuls from Italy to Eretz Yisrael. Perhaps they were inspired by the Medrash that states that in the days of Mashiach, *batei midrash* and shuls will be transported to the Holy Land. Today some of these shuls are museums while others are in actual use.

Words from the Wise

When the Ponovezher Rav was once in Rome he asked that they take him to see the Arch of Titus. As he gazed up at the huge structure, he shook his fist and said, “Titus, Titus, where are you? I am here but there is nothing left of the Roman Empire ….”

The magnificent golden *aron kodesh* that graces the Ponovezher Yeshivah was built in the seventeenth century for the main shul of Mantua, Italy. The *aron kodesh* was carefully taken apart and put into storage during the Second World War. Skilled workers in Bnei Brak later put the *aron kodesh* together from hundreds of pieces that were imported from Mantua, rebuilding the magnificent original.

The Ponovezher Rav

The Italian Alps

What's the Weather?

Most of Italy has a pleasant climate with warm dry summers and mild winters. Occasionally, a warm, humid wind called the sirocco blows from North Africa. Rainfall is heaviest in the north near the Alps. Most Italians live close to one of Italy's two towering mountain ranges, the Alps and the Apennines, so skiing is very popular.

Italy's Wildlife

In Italy's remote wild places and in its many national parks, animals such as the brown bear can still enjoy wilderness largely untouched by humans. Italy is home to some of Europe's last population of wild animals, such as the wolves and the goat-like chamois.

Chamois

Gray wolf

Brown bear

Did you know that Italy's main agricultural products are wine, olive oil, fruits, vegetables, beef, fish, and dairy?

Italy's other main industries are tourism and manufacturing.

Leaning Tower of Pisa

An eight-story tower in Italy called the Leaning Tower of Pisa has been leaning for over 800 years. It leans because the soil beneath it is too soft for such a heavy building. It contains 32 million pounds of marble. No wonder it is sinking!

Italy's Sages Throughout The Ages

Rav Ovadiah Bertinoro, who wrote the famous commentary on the *Mishnah* commonly known as the "Rav," was born in Italy in middle of the 15th century. When he was in his forties he decided to travel to Eretz Yisrael. It took him two years to get there! (Today, it is about a four-hour flight.) Rav Ovadiah became the Chief Rabbi of Yerushalayim. The Yerushalmi community was very poor, so Rav Ovadiah collected funds from his friends in Italy for the poor of Yerushalayim. It is a long-standing tradition of the Jews of the Diaspora — countries outside of Eretz Yisrael — to support communities in Eretz Yisrael.

Rav Ovadiah ben Yaakov Sforno was a Torah scholar and halachic authority. He was a doctor who supported himself by practicing medicine. At the same time he was a judge in the local *bais din*. He is most famous for his commentary on *Chumash*, which is still learned today. The Sforno, as he is known, was born in Italy and died there in 1550.

The kever of Rav Moshe Chaim Luzzato, the Ramchal, in Teveryah

The Rama MiPano, ***Rav Menachem Azariah***, was a Kabbalist who was born in 1548 in the Italian city of Fano. The Rama MiPano was a very wealthy man who lived in a magnificent palace. The Chida once said that Rav Menachem Azariah looked like an angel. Even though he was so wealthy, the Rama had one room in his palace that was called the "*galus* room." The room was bare and simple. He spent most of his time in this room, devoting day and night to Hashem and His holy Torah. The Rama MiPano died in 1620.

Rav Moshe Chaim Luzzato, famously known as Ramchal, was born in Padua, Italy in 1707. He was a great Kabbalist and Jewish philosopher. He authored many *sefarim*, including the *Mesillas Yesharim*, a classic *mussar sefer* studied to this day in yeshivos throughout the world. In 1743, he and his family left Italy for Eretz Yisrael and settled in the holy city of Teveryah. At the age of forty, he died in an epidemic that swept the city. He is buried in Teveryah next to the grave of Rabbi Akiva.

Italy's flag is green, white, and red. The Italians wanted to show their support to the French emperor Napoleon, whose favorite color was green. They therefore included a green stripe on the flag.

Two Famous Jews Who Visited Italy and the Rest of the World

Binyamin of Tudela was a famous Jewish traveler at a time when people hardly ever left their villages. He lived in the 12th century and traveled through Europe, Asia, and Africa. He wrote about his travels, and described the many Jewish communities he encountered in Italy.

The Chida, **Rav Chaim Yosef David Azulai**, was one of the *gedolei hador* in the 1700s. He wrote more than twenty *sefarim*. He was born in Eretz Yisrael. He traveled all through Europe to raise money for the community in Chevron. He brought a little bit of the holiness of Eretz Yisrael to all the communities in Italy that he visited.

Did you know that there is a tiny country called Vatican City inside the city of Rome?

Although it has never been poven, some say that the Menorah and other holy vessels from the *Beis HaMikdash* are hidden in vaults under the Vatican.

The kever of Rav Chaim Yosef David Azulai, the Chida, on Har HaMenuchos

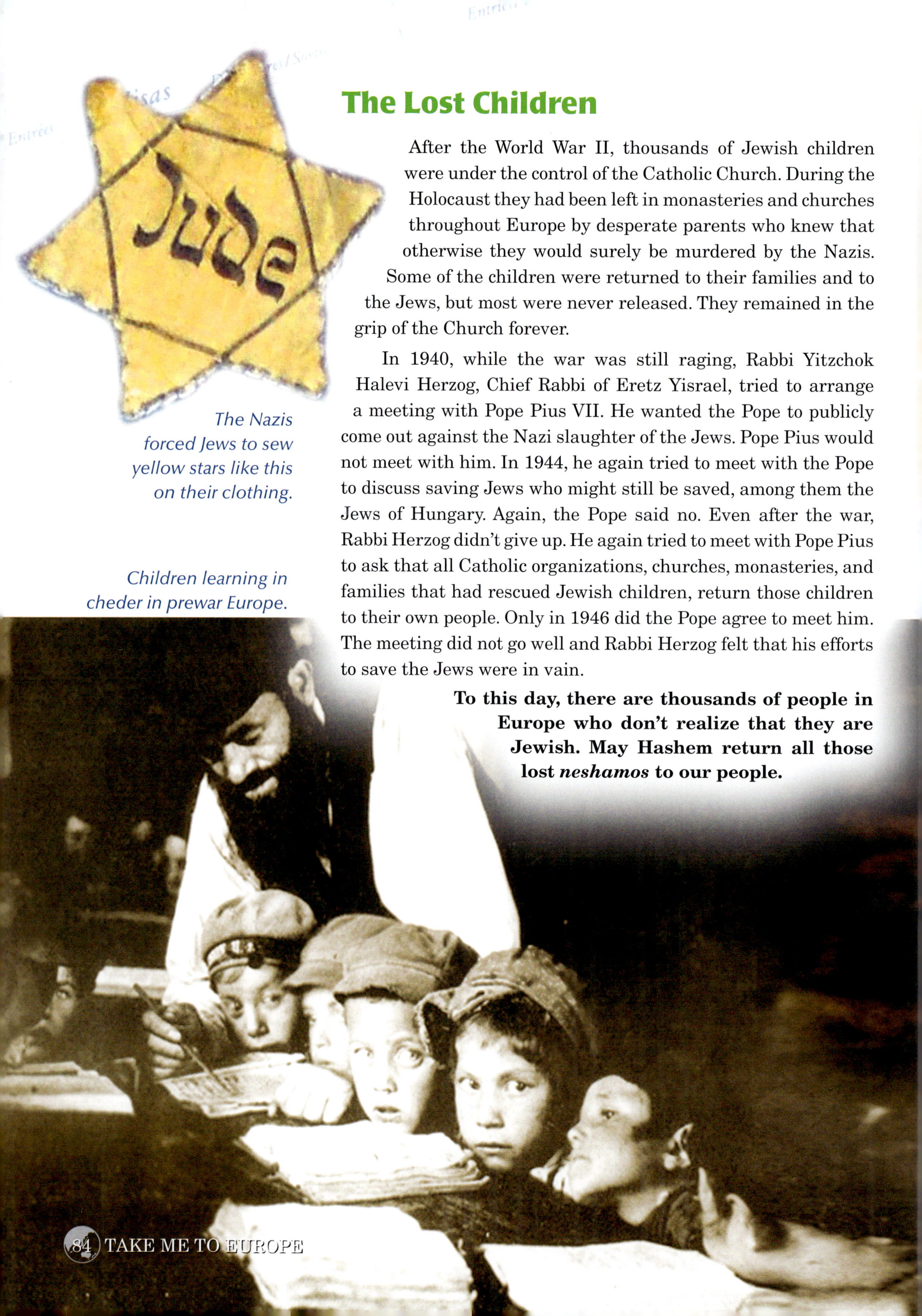

The Nazis forced Jews to sew yellow stars like this on their clothing.

The Lost Children

After the World War II, thousands of Jewish children were under the control of the Catholic Church. During the Holocaust they had been left in monasteries and churches throughout Europe by desperate parents who knew that otherwise they would surely be murdered by the Nazis. Some of the children were returned to their families and to the Jews, but most were never released. They remained in the grip of the Church forever.

In 1940, while the war was still raging, Rabbi Yitzchok Halevi Herzog, Chief Rabbi of Eretz Yisrael, tried to arrange a meeting with Pope Pius VII. He wanted the Pope to publicly come out against the Nazi slaughter of the Jews. Pope Pius would not meet with him. In 1944, he again tried to meet with the Pope to discuss saving Jews who might still be saved, among them the Jews of Hungary. Again, the Pope said no. Even after the war, Rabbi Herzog didn't give up. He again tried to meet with Pope Pius to ask that all Catholic organizations, churches, monasteries, and families that had rescued Jewish children, return those children to their own people. Only in 1946 did the Pope agree to meet him. The meeting did not go well and Rabbi Herzog felt that his efforts to save the Jews were in vain.

To this day, there are thousands of people in Europe who don't realize that they are Jewish. May Hashem return all those lost *neshamos* to our people.

Children learning in cheder in prewar Europe.

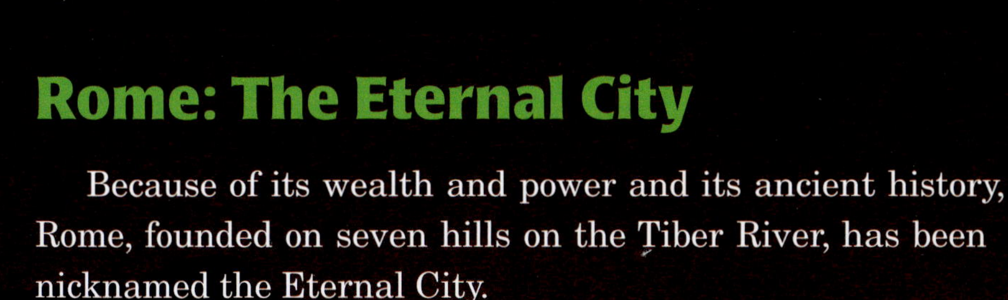

Rome: The Eternal City

Because of its wealth and power and its ancient history, Rome, founded on seven hills on the Tiber River, has been nicknamed the Eternal City.

We, however, know that this eternity will come to an abrupt end the minute Hashem wills it.

Story Corner

The Four Captives

Toward the end of the 10th century, four Babylonian *chachamim* left Italy on a trip to raise funds for the yeshivos of their country. The ship they traveled on set sail from Bari, Italy, and it was soon captured by a Spanish pirate. Knowing that the Jews always try to save their people, the wicked pirate approached Jewish communities in four different countries to demand a huge ransom for these famous captives. Each prisoner was redeemed by a different community.

Rav Shemaria was ransomed by the Jewish community in Alexandria, Egypt. He started a successful yeshivah in Cairo. Rav Chushiel, father of Rabeinu Chananel, was ransomed by the Jews of Tunisia. He founded a thriving yeshivah in Kairouan. Rav Moshe was ransomed in Cordoba, Spain, where he, too, established a yeshivah. The identity of the fourth captive is unknown.

These captives became known as the *Arba Shevuyim*, or four captives. Each of these great men started yeshivos and thriving Torah centers. It can be said that from Italy, Torah was spread throughout the civilized world.

What seemed to be a tragedy turned out to be something very good for the Jewish people. Truly Hashem works in wondrous ways.

1

2

1. *In the late 19th century, Cristoforo Benigno Crespi a textile manufacturer, established a community for his employees in Lombardy, Italy. His family home is known as the Castle of Crespi. The village is still inhabited by descendants of the original mill workers.*
2. *These conical homes, the Trulli di Alberolbello, in Italy, are built in a traditional style without using mortar.*
3. *The largest palm grove in Europe is the Palmeral of Elche in Spain. More than 11,000 trees are found in the Palmeral; some are 300 years old!*
4. *Alhambra, in Granada, Spain, was used as a palace by Moorish rulers in the 14th century. It was called "a pearl set in emeralds" because of its light stone walls set amid green forests.*

3

4

5

6

5. St. Pancras Railway Station, known for its Victorian architecture, has tracks to France and Belgium. Happy traveling!
6. The tallest Ferris wheel in Europe, the London Eye is 443 feet tall and almost 400 feet in diameter! Don't get dizzy!
7. The ancient Romans built the Pont du Gard aqueduct in France to bring water across 31 miles to the city of Nimes. After the aqueduct was no longer used to carry water, it was a toll bridge for hundreds of years. Now it is a tourist attraction—but don't try to drive your car over it!
8. The Chateau Fontainebleau, near Paris, France, has been a royal residence for over 700 years! It has more than 1500 rooms and is surrounded by parks and gardens.

7

8

Conclusion

The Jewish nation has spoken many languages and has inhabited nearly every corner of the globe. We have lived in peace and persecution, freedom and slavery, and have adopted the different customs of our host countries. One of the stops on the long and difficult journey of exile was Europe. Our people lived in Europe for over a thousand years. European soil is saturated with Jewish blood. Crusades, pogroms, blood libels, autos-da-fé, and the Holocaust all took place in Europe. At the same time, Europe was also witness to the glory of our nation. Many of the major Jewish works — *sefarim* of some of our greatest *gedolim* in the past thousand years were written in Europe. Many great yeshivos and citadels of Torah dotted the landscape of Eastern and Western Europe.

It is the Torah that is the bridge that has spanned thousands of years of Jewish history. No matter where you live, dear reader, as long as you learn our holy Torah and live by its dictates, you are connected to every other Jew, past, present, and future. You are part of a glorious nation with a glorious heritage. We are all children of *HaKadosh Baruch Hu*, Master of the World, King of all kings. The entire world is the footstool of our Creator. We can hardly wait for the day when the entire world will be filled with the knowledge of Hashem. Until that day, in whatever corner of the globe we inhabit, let us remain connected to our heritage and our nation through the Torah, upon which the entire world exists.

Mesorah Publications, ltd
4401 Second Avenue
Brooklyn, New York 11232
(718) 921-9000
www.artscroll.com

UNITED KINGDOM
Hebrides
Orkney Is.
Bergen
Stavanger
Skagerrak
LANTIC
SCOTLAND
Aberdeen
Glasgow
Dundee
Edinburgh
N. IRELAND
Belfast
IRELAND
Dublin
Cork
North
Sea
DENMARK
Ålborg
Newcastle-upon-Tyne
Manchester
Leeds
Liverpool
Sheffield
Kiel
WALES
Birmingham
ENGLAND
Cardiff
Bristol
LONDON
Southampton
Plymouth
Amsterdam
The Hague
Rotterdam
NETHER-LANDS
Bremen
Hannover
Antwerp
BELGIUM
Essen
Dortmund
Cologne
Brussels
Bonn
CEAN
English Channel
Le Havre
Channel Is. (U.K.)
Lille
Brest
Rouen
Seine
PARIS
Luxembourg
LUX.
Frankfurt am Main
Nuremberg
Halle
Leipzig
FRANCE
Rhine
Strasbou
Stuttgart
Munich
Nantes
Dijon
Bay of Biscay
Gironde
Zürich
Bordeaux
La Coruña
Bilbao
Garonne
Milan
Turin
Genoa
Bologna
Venice
Toulous
ANDORRA
Valladolid
Douro
Madrid
Florence
SPAIN
Tagus
Guadiana
Barcelona
Ajaccio
Rome
Valencia
Balearic
Minorca
Sardinia
Palma
Ibiza
Majorca
Córdoba
Guadalquivir
Murcia
Alicante
Granada
Tyrrhenia
Sea
Cagliari